He arrived home again just before nine. There was a message from Foster to say that the navy would be on the job in the morning – weather permitting. He listened to the forecast. 'Continuing fine at first tomorrow, with long sunny periods, but rain will reach the south-west later in the day with strengthening winds.'

Was it too much to ask that for once a poor, struggling policeman might be favourably noticed by Providence?

W.J. Burley lived near Newquay in Cornwall, and was a schoolmaster until he retired to concentrate on his writing. His many Wycliffe books include, most recently, *Wycliffe and the Guild of Nine*. He died in 2002.

By W.J. Burley

Wycliffe's
WILD-GOOSE CHASE

W.J.Burley

AN ORION PAPERBACK

First published in Great Britain in 1982
by Victor Gollancz Ltd
First published in paperback in 1989
by Corgi Books
This paperback edition published in 2005
by Orion Books Ltd
Orion House, 5 Upper St Martin's Lane,
London WC2H 9EA

An Hachette Livre UK company

3 5 7 9 10 8 6 4 2

A CIP catalogue record for this book
is available from the British Library.

ISBN 978-0-7528-6491-4

Printed and bound in Great Britain by
Clays Ltd, St Ives plc

The Orion Publishing Group's policy is to use papers that
are natural, renewable and recyclable products and
made from wood grown in sustainable forests. The logging
and manufacturing processes are expected to conform to
the environmental regulations of the country of origin.

www.orionbooks.co.uk

CHAPTER ONE

Thursday evening. Outside it was raining. The three men sat round the fire in well-worn leather armchairs. Smoke rose from their pipes and drifted along the ceiling between the beams. On the high mantelpiece an alarm clock in a shiny metal case ticked the seconds away, clink-clink, clink-clink . . . Each man had a glass at hand; the major was drinking whisky, the other two, white wine. The room was clean and warm but bare, like a farm kitchen. Apart from the three armchairs there was a large, square kitchen table and four bentwood chairs; there was fibre matting on the floor and a three-legged crock for a coal-scuttle. On the wall opposite the fireplace tiers of shelves were crammed with a tattered collection of books, many of them lacking a spine and therefore anonymous.

Bunny Lane reached for the bottle of white wine which he had placed behind his chair, away from the heat of the fire. 'Can I top you up, Joseph?' Bunny was so called because he had a hare-lip which a black moustache failed to hide and when he spoke his words came with a sibilant whistle.

Joseph, the red-head, held out his glass, 'Thanks.'

Bunny made his own wine, largely from grapes which he grew in the lean-to greenhouse behind the kitchen. 'You all right, Major?'

The major sat back in his chair, his legs stretched to the fire. He was massively built with machine-clipped grey hair which accentuated the Teutonic mould of his skull. He looked at the whisky glass in his hand and said in a gravelly voice, 'I'm well enough.' He had grey eyes which bulged slightly and a steady disconcerting stare.

The fire glowed orange-red with a flicker of flame whenever the coals settled. The major sipped his whisky and sighed; Joseph, the red-head, re-lit his pipe which had gone out. The alarm clock kept up its insistent clink-clink. It was twenty minutes past eight.

Bunny Lane said, 'How are things with you, Joseph?'

Joseph did not answer at once, he smoked his pipe and seemed to be considering. In the end he said, 'I don't know.' Then, after a long pause he added, 'I'm just waiting . . .' He made an irritable movement which caused the springs of the old chair to creak. 'I wish to God I'd never agreed to take him in with me!'

The major turned his grey eyes on Joseph. 'Ah!'

Joseph stared into the fire. 'It can't go on much longer . . . One way or the other . . .'

This was followed by a silence which must have lasted all of five minutes. It was as though they felt the need to atone for such prodigality with words. Bunny rose from his chair and with a pair of tongs took several lumps of coal from the crock and placed them carefully on the fire, then he resumed his seat. The major was the first to speak again.

'What do you say to a game?' He moved round in his chair so that his gaze rested on the box of dominoes which stood ready in the middle of the wooden table.

Without a word the other two got to their feet and, carrying their glasses, moved to the bentwood chairs. The major joined them, towering over the table for a moment before sitting down. Then came the rattle of the dominoes being tipped from their box, the shuffling, the draw, and the silence while they considered their hands. They played with a minimum of words. From time to time Bunny got up to see to the fire or to recharge their glasses. There was a longer interruption

6

while he opened a fresh bottle of wine. The major continued to drink whisky to which he added very little water and as the evening wore on his movements became slower and more deliberate though no less precise and his eyes lost all trace of expression. The only sounds came from the placing of the dominoes, the clink-clink of the alarm clock and occasional crepitations from the fire.

At twenty minutes to eleven, when they had finished a game, the major stood up and, carefully enunciating his words, said, 'I must be going; I wish you both good-night.'

Joseph got up from his chair, 'I'll come with you, Major.'

Bunny saw them to the door. It was still raining. In the tiny front passage the major struggled into his duffle coat but went bareheaded; Joseph put on his fawn raincoat and tweed hat. They muttered good-nights then set off together, Joseph's stocky figure dwarfed by the major's bulk.

Bunny Lane's little house and his workshop formed part of a square of terraced houses. The two men came out of the square and turned down the hill towards Bear Street with the rain driving in their faces. Bear Street, a narrow, ill-lit shopping street was deserted. Joseph stood by his antique shop and let himself in by the side-door.

'Good-night, Major.'

'Good-night! Good-night to you, Joseph.'

The major continued along the street then turned up Dog's Leg Lane towards Garrison Drive.

Hetty Lloyd Parkyn, the major's sister, was in her little sitting-room, sandwiched between the drawing-room and the kitchen. It was a long time since they had used the drawing-room – certainly not since the death of their father. Hetty had her sitting-room on one side of the passage, Gavin's was on the other. Hetty's would have seemed shabby and bleak to a lonely old maid struggling to survive on her pension. The upholstery of the two armchairs was so worn that no pattern was discernible, the carpet was threadbare and the curtains sagged where hooks had come adrift. She sat in one of the armchairs, reading, and placed near her chair was an old-fashioned oil-stove with a red window and a fretted top which gave off a moist, smelly heat.

Hetty was tall and big-boned like her brother, but lean and gaunt; her hair and eyes were grey and her skin seemed to have been bleached of all natural colour. As she read she reached out from time to time to a paper bag of white peppermints.

Somewhere in the house a clock struck eleven and almost at once her sharp ears caught a sound from the back of the house; she heard a door open and shut, a key turn and a bolt shoot home. A moment or two later there were footsteps in the passage, the door of her room opened, and her brother's great bulk almost filled the doorway. His grey hair was darkened by rain, droplets of water stood out on the coarse material of his duffle coat and water dripped from his trousers to the floor.

He stood without speaking, gazing at his sister with expressionless eyes.

Hetty scarcely looked up from her book. 'There's some soup in the saucepan on the stove if you care to heat it up.'

The major turned away, closing the door behind him. She heard him fumbling about in the hall, removing his coat; then heavy slow footsteps on the stairs; he was on his way to bed.

Two nights later – Saturday evening – Joseph Clement sat at his desk by a first-floor window which overlooked the backyard of his house and shop and the backyards of

8

neighbouring houses in Bear Street. Outside, in the leaden dusk, rain fell vertically, unhurried and unremitting. Joseph's room had the unmistakable aura of a cell, a place of refuge from the world. It was a bedsitter, not because of a shortage of rooms in the house, but because Joseph chose to spend as much of his time as possible ensconced with his stamps, his albums and catalogues, his books on English furniture and his notes for a projected history of philately.

The yellow light from a naked bulb fell on his red hair and on a little heap of stamps, each in its polythene envelope: a selection from the early issues of Guatemala, sent to him by a correspondent there. He picked up his forceps and magnifier and bent his head to the task of examining them. But the thrill of the chase was lacking for he had not yet succeeded in shutting out his troubles from the little room, they trailed after him as inexorably as Marley's train of cash-boxes. He persevered because he knew that in the end he would become absorbed; the atmosphere of his burrow would work on him as surely as a sedative drug and he would recapture something of the contentment which, not so long ago, he had accepted as his normal state of being.

He was pleased with two surcharged *quetzal* stamps of 1881, they were not valuable but they filled a gap in his collection; and by three rarer values in the commemoratives for the Central American Exhibition of 1897, one with an unrecorded flaw in the portrait of Barrios.

His breathing settled to a gentle, regular rhythm, his thick fingers which had red hairs on their backs manipulated the stamps with an acquired skill; the slightly humid stuffiness of the room enveloped him and the little clock on his desk ticked the seconds away. It grew darker outside until the window panes were shining black squares. Fifteen minutes to eight.

A buzzer sounded in the passage, someone at the side-door. Joseph got up with a sigh, pushing back his chair. He moved heavily, ponderously, in the manner of an older, bigger man. He was forty-five and though stockily built, by no means fat. He went out into the passage, down the stairs, and opened the side-door. A man in a mackintosh stood there, clutching a leather bag, his shoulders hunched against the rain.

'I'm Waddington, I've come to see Dave Clement; he's expecting me.'

The man made a move to come in and Joseph reluctantly stood aside. 'You'd better come through the shop to the office.' He closed the side-door and opened another which led into the dark cavern of the shop. 'This way!' Without putting on any lights Joseph threaded his way through the stock-in-trade of the antique shop to the office at the back but it was only when he switched on the light there that Waddington was able to follow him.

Waddington came blinking out of the darkness, a weedy specimen, long and lank and sallow as though grown in a poor light. Yet he must have cared for his appearance for the narrow bands of hair which linked sideburns to moustache had been lovingly cultivated. He looked round the office with suspicion. 'Where's Dave?'

'He's out at the moment but I'm expecting him back.'

David Clement stood naked in the shower, sponging himself. He was as unlike his brother as could be imagined, slight of build, very dark, with small bones and delicate features which were almost feminine. He was on the wrong side of thirty while the girl on the bed had several years to go.

'What's the rush tonight?' She put her legs over the side of the bed and sat watching him, scratching her breasts and yawning.

'Waddy is coming at eight.'

'*Waddy*? What does he want?'

Clement reached for a towel. 'I don't know but I can guess.'

'Can he make trouble?'

'Only for himself; he's a stupid bastard.'

'You won't let them talk you out of it?'

'No chance!' He came over and stood by her, rubbing himself down. 'I've told you, Mo, I'm getting out and there's nothing they or anybody else can do to stop me now.'

'How soon?'

'A month? Six weeks? There's no great rush, is there? One or two things I've got to do – flog *Manna* for a start, but I've already put an advert in next week's issue of *Power Boat* and there should be plenty of offers. Boats like *Manna* don't hang about this time of year.'

The girl continued to look worried. 'Is Waddy coming off his own bat or has he been sent?'

Clement shrugged. 'Probably it's Chalky's doing. Chalky is a shit but he knows too well which side his bread is buttered to try anything on.'

Clement pulled on his briefs and reached for his shirt. The girl got off the bed and walked to the shower; she put on a shower cap and tucked in her long, dark hair. 'Shall I see you tomorrow?'

'I thought I'd spend the day on the boat, Mo – get her into shape for a possible buyer.'

'Pick me up, I'll come with you.'

'You're on nights; you need your beauty sleep.'

She paused in the act of reaching for the shower tap. 'It's not the boat is it? It's some bloody girl!'

'Don't be stupid, Mo!'

'Then pick me up like I said.'

'We'll see.'

Clement was dressed, he ran a comb through his hair in front of the dressing-table mirror. 'I must be off; I don't want Waddy opening his big mouth to brother Joseph.'

Clement left the bedroom, passed through the tiny sitting-room to the box-like hall where his wet mackintosh hung on a peg, put it on and let himself out of the flat.

In Godolphin Street the rain fell steadily. Keeping close to the houses he walked the length of the street then turned left into Bear Street where the narrow roadway gleamed in patches under the street lamps and the only sign of life came from a brightly lit restaurant opposite the antique shop.

Through the windows of the antique shop Clement could see a faint glow of light from the office at the back. He let himself in by the side-door and moved soundlessly through the shop so that he was standing in the doorway of the office before either Joseph or Waddington realized that he was there. Joseph was sitting on one side of the big desk, Waddington on the other and between them, laid out on the blotter, were six paper-weights which reflected the light of the lamp in a glowing spectrum of colour.

David said, 'Hullo, Waddy! Got something pretty to sell?'

Sunday. After a cold, wet and blustery fortnight it seemed quite possible that spring had arrived; the air was soft and the waters of the estuary dazzled the eyes with scintillating reflections of the low sun. Soon, God and weather permitting, the Wycliffes would be having friends out to admire their camellias, magnolias, azaleas and rhododendrons. Then, in a little while, there would be the occasional meal out-of-doors and they would spend long evenings working in the garden and go to bed dog-tired but with the comfortable feeling that they had in some way put themselves right with the world.

There was no other house in sight on their side of the estuary and so they had a hoard of privacy, the real hard currency of the century. In these days a half-acre of shrubs and trees may give one feelings of guilt or delusions of grandeur, either way the Wycliffes had made up their minds not to be over-run by the lemmings if they could help it. Sometimes he experienced a twinge from his socialist, non-conformist conscience but Helen was made of sterner stuff.

Half-past seven. They were early risers even on Sundays for no day was long enough for Helen. In her dressing-gown she turned the pages of a gardening magazine while she nibbled her toast and marmalade. (A fat-free breakfast with black coffee.)

Wycliffe said, 'I think I'll walk along the shore and collect the newspapers.' He usually did on fine Sunday mornings.

There were more and more things which they usually did, for their domestic life was beginning to gel now that child raising was over. He was forty-nine, an age at which a man must admit that, technically at least, he is over the hill. The twins were gone – flown almost literally from the nest. David jetted about on behalf of some quasi-governmental agency dispensing scientific largesse to the Third World: Nepal, Ecuador, Lesotho . . . not forgetting regular get-togethers in the Eurocaps. Ruth was almost as mobile. As her boss's personal assistant she regularly trailed him around Europe and to the States; she had been twice to Tokyo and once to the Gulf. And the twins were still only in their middle twenties, about the age at which he had first crossed the channel – by car-ferry – feeling a bit like Captain Cook and wondering if he really could drive on the right.

The upshot of it all was that he and Helen were alone again, and liking it, though mildly disturbed by questions. What had it all been about? Where do we go from here? Why did we . . . ? Perhaps understanding for the first time that this is the real thing – not a dress rehearsal. At any rate he was untroubled by professional ambition; he had climbed as high as he wanted to go – higher, he

sometimes thought. The arid plateau of pure adminis-
tration had no allure; not for him the plush office
behind the padded door.

People who knew his background thought he had
done well. Son of a Hertfordshire tenant farmer, starting
as a trainee copper at nineteen, he had become detective chief superintendent and head of C.I.D. for two
counties. Yet he was vaguely dissatisfied; secretly he saw
himself as a failure. Where did it all lead? To a pension,
an up-market bit of silver and, perhaps, an O.B.E. From
one day to the next . . .

'See if they've got any white-wine vinegar at the shop,
I've run out.'

The village of St Juliot was a mile or so further up the
estuary from the Watch House where the Wycliffes
lived; nearer the city. Wycliffe let himself out by a little
gate at the bottom of the garden, crossed a rarely used
public footpath, and dropped a couple of feet to the
shingle beach. At this point the opposite shore of the
estuary was only a few hundred yards away and through
this bottleneck all the shipping of the busy port had to
pass.

Half-an-hour since low water. Oyster catchers
explored the muddy margins of the tide and further
down the estuary a colony of lesser black-backs, uni-
formly spaced, faced whatever breeze there was and
waited, Micawber-like.

Familiarity did not breed contempt but it dulled the
edge of perception. He needed to remind himself from
time to time how lucky they were to live in such
surroundings and still be within twenty or thirty
minutes' drive of his headquarters.

He followed the line of high-water where a tangle of
drying wrack was mixed with plastic rubbish and an
occasional gobbet of black oil. Pollution troubled him
but he tried not to think about it; there were a few things
he could do something about, better to think of them.

14

Near the village, where the long narrow back-gardens of the cottages reached the shore, there was a row of upturned dinghies, hauled well above the tide line. Offshore a dozen or more pleasure craft rode at moorings and in a month there would be many more. Beyond St Juliot, still further up the estuary, the city sprawled over its creeks and hills, snug and smug when international squabbles were settled by cannon balls; now, almost entirely rebuilt after a war with aircraft and bombs and asking itself, What next?

At the end of the village there was a quay, once used for shipping stone from a quarry now derelict. A few yards short of the quay something gleamed in the shingle, not far below high-water mark. As he crunched towards it he saw that it was a gun ... a revolver ... service pattern from the last war ... a .38. He picked it up gingerly and sniffed. Recently fired? He thought so, and still loaded in some chambers. The catch was on.

Many times in recent years he had complained that rank cut him off from the early stages of an investigation. 'You come in when the show is half over.' Not in this case; he was in at the start and he could imagine the headline in the local paper: 'C.I.D. Chief Finds Gun On Beach.'

With a bit of string from his pocket he slung the gun from the trigger guard. Although he had found it below the tide-mark the gun had never been in the sea. High tide had been at one in the morning and it would have taken about an hour to fall to where he had found the gun; so, it must have been dropped there at some time after two – within the previous six hours.

Wycliffe took guns very seriously; he did not like them. A man could be blasted out of existence because of some cretin's panic or anger or hatred. Bang! You're dead! And all the King's horses and all the King's men can't put Humpty together again.

He looked around. No sign of any disturbance in the

shingle but that was hardly surprising, he could not pick out his own tracks.

He climbed the granite steps of the quay, steps that were slimy with bottle-green weed at the bottom and encrusted with grey and orange lichens near the top. Except by going through one of the terraced cottages there was no other way off the beach. Grass pushed up between the stonework of the surface of the quay, making its own thin carpet of soil. At the seaward end four broken-off cast-iron pillars were all that remained of a mechanical contraption for loading stone into ships.

Near the pillars he found three places where the grass had been crushed – as it might have been by the wheels of a parked car or van. Where the fourth wheel would have rested there was no grass to take an impression, only smooth stone. The quay was reached by a lane off the St Juliot road; the lane had once been used by trucks and was still passable in a car. At the shoreward end of the quay there was a turning space and a confusion of wheel marks but no obviously identifiable tread.

The church bell tolled for early communion – the tenor bell, slightly cracked. In the lane, after a fortnight of rain, there was a great deal of black mud, too soft to retain any impression. The lane joined a minor road which, coming from the general direction of the city, meandered through St Juliot, on past the Watch House, to the coast.

Outside his shop Tommy Carne, a dark haired, stocky, pre-Celtic Briton, worked with the energy of the self-employed, unpacking his parcels of newspapers.

'Good morning, Mr Wycliffe! You're a bit early but give me a couple of minutes.'

Too busy to notice whether the superintendent carried a gun or a parasol.

The vicar in his cassock crossed from the vicarage to the church as the bell stopped tolling and raised his hands in distant acknowledgement of a lost sheep. The village was coming to life, curtains were drawn back in upstair rooms, dogs were let out to make their morning rounds, the sluggish Sunday routine was getting under way.

There was a telephone box on a triangle of grass in front of the shop. Wycliffe propped the gun on a ledge while he dialled and fed in a coin.

'Police Headquarters.'

'Superintendent Wycliffe. Give me C.I.D., please.'

'Detective Sergeant Kersey.'

Kersey was a recent acquisition from one of the city divisions, a man who had stuck at sergeant because he concerned himself more with the job than with promotion. Wycliffe was nursing him for a belated reward.

'Any shooting during the night?'

'Nothing in the report, sir.'

'Who is with you?'

'Dixon and Potter.'

'Send them out here to me. Dixon can use a camera so get him to bring one. Call Smithy at home and ask him to meet me in my office as soon as possible, then check this hand-gun with Records – a Webley and Scott, service-pattern revolver . . . '

He made a second call, this time to Helen.

'It's me; something's cropped up.'

'In the village?'

'I found a loaded revolver on the beach. I'll ring later.'

He walked back to the corner of the lane to wait for his men.

If the gun had been fired on the beach or the quay it would have been heard in the village. Even a car driven along the lane at night would have attracted attention. St Juliot nights are serenely peaceful and St Juliot people extremely nosy.

A little girl came out of a nearby house and stood staring up at him with unblinking brown eyes; she had a

17

well gnawed rusk in one hand which she seemed to have forgotten about. A milk float rattled by, bottles and crates clinking. The patrol car arrived with a uniformed driver and Dixon and Potter got out, sniffing the air, wondering whether it offered anything more entertaining than playing cards in the duty room. Wycliffe told them what he wanted and left them to it, then he was driven to headquarters in the patrol car.

The building was wrapped in Sunday morning calm. No typewriters tapped, no telephones rang and the desk sergeant was reading the *Sunday Mirror* with a mug of tea at his elbow. An enquiry which breaks on a Sunday gets off to a slow start because policemen like other mortals want to do their Sunday thing; gardening, fishing, sleeping, taking the kids and dogs for walks, even going to church.

Sergeant Smith joined Wycliffe in his office. Smith had been a member of the headquarters crime squad since before the Wycliffe era, first as a general duties officer and part-time photographer; more recently, after an extended Home Office course, as full-time photographer and finger-print expert. Everything about Smith was grey; clothes, skin, hair and personality, but he was good at his job as long as it kept him away from people; people and Smithy did not mix.

He looked at the gun without touching it while Wycliffe explained. 'They're checking with Records.'

'They won't find anything. Too many of these about – souvenirs of the war. People get worried and ditch them in daft places – ought to have another amnesty.'

'Five chambers loaded and, I'd guess, one recently fired.'

Smith's shaggy eyebrows, like miniature horns, went up. 'Any overnight brawls?'

'Nothing reported. I want you to go over it for prints then send it to Melville.'

Melville was a ballistics expert attached to forensic.

18

Smith looked his surprise. He thought Wycliffe was making a mountain out of a molehill but he also thought that it wasn't his place to say so, which was one of the aggravating things about Smith. He went off with the gun which left a faint oily stain on Wycliffe's blotter.

He thought, Nobody would go to St Juliot to dispose of an unwanted, even an incriminating gun; a gun is small enough to be got rid of unobtrusively amost anywhere, by burying it, throwing it in the river or the sea, even down a street drain.

A body is a different matter, especially if one doesn't want to see it again. But contrary to common belief it is not easy to dispose of a body even in the sea. It has to go into deep water at the right state of the tide and for this one needs a pier or quay – often conspicuous places – or a boat. Wycliffe picked up the telephone and asked to be put through to the harbour master.

'I don't suppose he will be in his office on a Sunday morning so try his home.'

It took a couple of minutes.

'Mr Foster? . . . Wycliffe, C.I.D.' The two men had met at several civic bunfights. 'Sorry to bother you on a Sunday morning . . .'

'Think nothing of it.'

'This is my problem: if you wanted to dispose of a body in the estuary and you weren't anxious to see it again, where would you choose?'

'Somewhere without too many coppers about.'

'All right, but where?'

'I'm thinking.' There was a longish pause before he spoke again. 'I can't think of a better place than the bottom of your garden.'

'But that's a shelving beach—'

'And you haven't got a boat, so if I were you I'd do the next best thing and push it off the end of the quay at St Juliot. If you lived the other side of the estuary I'd suggest Potter's Wharf but that's more overlooked.'

19

'Why those two places?'

'Because they're both near the entrance to the narrows and anything that goes in there at the right state of the ebb is swept out to sea at a rate of knots. You know that as well as I do.'

'You said, the right state of the ebb – when, exactly?'

Foster considered, muttering to himself. 'Beginning from an hour to an hour-and-a-half after high water and lasting for about two hours. The channel is scoured in that time.'

'And last night, for instance?'

The harbour master jibbed. 'Am I going to have to say all this in court?'

'It's possible, I suppose, but if you do I'll give you a chance to think again.'

A brief interval. 'Well, last night high water was at 00.48; there was a stiff breeze – five to six on the Beaufort scale – from the south-east but that wouldn't have affected conditions in the estuary much . . . I'd say the best time was between three and four in the morning.'

'Thanks. One more question: a body put in the water then, from the quay, would you expect to see it again?'

Foster hesitated. 'Not in the estuary, certainly; and nowhere else for quite a time but it would probably turn up further down the coast in the end – might be two or three weeks later, might be only a couple of days. You know what the sea is, everything depends on winds and currents and they're as unpredictable as women.' Foster had three unmarried daughters living at home.

So it made sense for someone with a body on his hands to drive out to St Juliot to get rid of it off the quay. A body . . . His imagination was running away with him. All he had was a gun with five of its six chambers loaded.

The telephone rang; a man from Records. 'You asked about a hand-gun, sir, a revolver—'

'Hold on while I get a pad.'

'The certificate was issued to Lieutenant-General Sir

20

Gavin Lloyd Parkyn of 3 Garrison Drive and it was last renewed three years ago. Shortly after that there was a break-in at the house and the gun was stolen along with certain valuables.'

'Ammunition?'

'None specified, sir. It was a souvenir weapon.'

Wycliffe had a vague recollection of the Garrison Drive case though he had not been involved. A collection of Japaneserie worth several thousand pounds. At the time he had been on secondment to an inquiry in the north of England, an unsavoury affair involving a senior police officer. He would have to dig in the files.

He turned to the bookshelves. In the field of military knights *Who's Who* never lets you down.

'Lloyd Parkyn, Lt-Gen. Sir Gavin . . . ' His date of birth was given as 1893 which would make him eighty-eight but Wycliffe's *Who's Who* was out of date so the old gentleman might have already passed on. A string of decorations and a record of war service in France and Germany during both wars, 'one *s*. one *dau*.' His wife died in 1950.

The next entry concerned the one *s*. 'Lloyd Parkyn, Maj. (R.M.) Gavin, C.B.E. (1970) D.S.O. (1952) and bar (1952); only *s* of Lt-Gen. Sir Gavin Lloyd Parkyn . . . b,1924; educ. Malvern, King's Coll. Cambridge . . . '

A distinguished family, bordering on the eminent.

It occurred to him that Kersey, before joining his headquarters squad, had been with B Division which included Garrison Drive so it was possible that he had worked on the break-in.

He found Kersey in the duty room in Sunday isolation; a cigarette stuck in one corner of his mouth, jabbing away at a typewriter like a hen pecking at corn. Wycliffe sat astride one of the chairs, his arms resting on the back.

'Do you know the Parkyns of Garrison Drive?'

Kersey gave him a wry look. 'The Major – I know him well enough and I've met his sister, Hetty.'

21

'And father?'

'Father had already passed on when I first came across them a couple of years ago. They had a break-in, lost a lot of Japanese stuff and a gun. Funny business.'

'Why funny?'

'Because it was a one-off job. You usually have a run – a gang working an area. Here there was no repeat performance. We didn't get anywhere, neither did Crime Squad.'

'Was the stuff valuable?'

'Twenty thousand or thereabouts.'

'Insured?'

'As far as I remember – not. Of course, the gun worried us but I don't think it ever turned up.'

'It has now.'

Kersey registered surprise. 'The gun on the beach? Well I'm damned!' He sat back in his chair to digest the news. 'So it could have been local after all; we put it down to a flying visit from the Smoke.'

'I think the gun had been recently fired.'

Kersey crushed his cigarette in a tin lid. 'No dabs I suppose?'

'Smith is checking but I'd be surprised if there were.'

'So would I. In that case there's nowhere to start, is there?'

Although Kersey had been attached to Wycliffe's squad for such a short time there was an easy relationship between the two men. From time to time Kersey threw in the odd 'sir' as a gesture to the hierarchy.

Wycliffe said, 'I suppose the place to start is where you left off – with the Parkyns.'

Kersey agreed. 'I suppose so but I doubt if it will get us far. As I remember we had job enough the first time. I felt like I was talking to myself in a padded cell.'

'We'll try again. At least they're entitled to know that part of their property has been recovered.'

'You want me to come with you, sir?'

'I haven't got a car, we can use yours.'

Kersey said, 'The sister, Hetty, is a recluse; I don't think she ever goes out. But every morning you can see the major bowling along Bear Street in his blue jersey and corduroys, carrying his little string bag. If it's wet or cold he wears an old service duffle coat. His first visit is to collect the paper to see what gee-gees are running, then he looks in on his old pal at the antique shop; after that the betting shop, then it's the butcher, the baker, and for all I know, the candle-stick maker – it wouldn't surprise me; the last time I was in the house on Garrison Drive it was full of smelly oil-stoves. Anyway, Parkyn is a well-known figure in the district – a character, as they say.'

'He bets over the counter?'

'Yes, but as I hear it only on horses with at least one wooden leg a-piece.' Kersey cackled. 'A bookmaker's charity – as though they needed one.'

They drove into the city centre and out in the direction of the old harbour to Bear Street. A quarter past twelve. Although the sun shone there were few people about, just the soberly dressed elect returning from church to their Sunday roast cooked by automatic timer.

Bear Street had been the principal thoroughfare of the Elizabethan town, now it meandered narrowly and aimlessly on the fringe of the modern city to end at the old harbour. Coveted by developers and fiercely defended by conservationists, Bear Street was fought over with no holds barred. Half-way along they turned up Dog's Leg Lane, between houses which were a last remnant of the first Elizabeth. The lane climbed steeply and, after the double twist which gave it its name, came out on the glacis of a great fort. The fort straddled the narrow neck of land which was all that separated the estuary from the sea at this point.

On this former glacis, with an effect of startling

incongruity, Victorian military engineers had built a row of large, detached red-brick houses for the senior officers of the garrison and their families. Architecturally they resembled block-houses but they were surrounded by pleasant gardens which sloped down the glacis, and the view was magnificent; the whole expanse of Porthellin Bay with the great crooked arm of Laira Head on the far side and the little village of Porthellin crouched in its shelter.

In contrast with the others the third house was sadly neglected. The garden was a jungle, the gates were off their hinges and the path up the garden to the front door was made hazardous by pot-holes and crumbling steps.

Kersey said, 'It hasn't changed for the better.'

The door-bell was answered by a very large man in a seaman's jersey, corduroy slacks and slippers.

Wycliffe introduced himself and the sergeant. 'Major Gavin Lloyd Parkyn?'

'Yes, what do you want?' The gravelly voice made Wycliffe want to cough on his behalf.

So this was Major Gavin Lloyd Parkyn, Royal Marines, C.B.E., D.S.O. and bar. Middle fifties, hair machine clipped, large features and grey eyes which bulged slightly.

'You'd better come in.'

The drawing-room was dustily, shabbily elegant and never used. It had a cold, damp, neglected feel and smelled of dry rot. But there was a magnificent Turkish carpet with a Tree of Life design, deep leather armchairs, a grand piano – now almost certainly untuneable – and two massive cabinets displaying blue-and-white porcelain.

Parkyn offered them chairs but he remained standing by the window so that his bulk was silhouetted against the light. Kersey did not sit down either.

'A little over two years ago you had a break-in and, among other things, your father's service revolver was stolen.'

Parkyn let out a short guttural bark which could have been a laugh. ' "Among other things" is right! My father's Japanese collections which the old man had not thought it worth while to insure.'

'I came to tell you that the gun has been recovered – by chance. I found it on the beach this morning at St. Juliot. It was loaded and I think it had been recently fired.'

The grey eyes stared at him unblinking. 'What was it doing on the beach?'

'I've no idea but we shall have to try to find out and that means taking another look at the original theft.'

The massive shoulders lifted in a slow shrug. 'Yes. Well, I've no objection but I can't see you getting far. After all, you didn't the first time.'

Wycliffe said, 'You may remember that Sergeant Kersey was concerned in the original inquiry.'

Parkyn glanced at the sergeant without interest.

'Of course, I shall turn up the files on the case but I should like you to tell me what you can of the circumstances and I would like to see where the gun and the other missing objects were kept.'

Parkyn seemed about to make some objection but changed his mind. 'If you like. Come with me.'

His manner was neither patronizing nor condescending, merely indifferent. As a little boy before the war Wycliffe had known someone very like Parkyn – 'The Colonel' – the big landowner in the district where the Wycliffes had been tenant farmers. The Colonel had the same monumental presence, the same gravelly voice matured on whisky and cigars, the same protruding grey eyes, and, above all, the same air of unconscious, effortless superiority.

They followed Parkyn out of the room and down a long passage to the back of the house; a thin haze of blue smoke from over-heated fat came from the kitchen. Parkyn pushed open the door of a large room. 'My father's den.'

The outmoded word aptly described the room which had grown comfortably shabby round the personality of the old general; tailored to fit, like a snail's shell. It was dominated by his portrait in oils over the mantelpiece, full-length, in dress uniform. He resembled Parkyn but was leaner, more finely drawn, with an aesthetic cast of countenance and thinner lips below the close-clipped moustache. Under the portrait the general's medals and decorations were displayed in a glass case.

The top of a large mahogany desk was laid out with his morocco leather blotter, scuffed at the edges; his address book and engagement diary; a perpetual calendar on a lignum-vitae stand; a cut-glass pen-tray; a stand with headed paper and envelopes and a little travelling clock which ticked away as though its owner had only just left the room. Photographs of army occasions jostled for position on the walls and there were shelves of well-thumbed books – memoirs, biographies, works on oriental art – real reference books ante-dating the era of coffee-table glossies. A row of fat exercise books could have been the general's journal.

The place was a shrine. But what astonished Wycliffe was that it had been kept spotlessly clean; every surface shone.

Parkyn said, 'He kept his Japanese stuff in that cabinet which he had specially made.'

It was a tall rosewood cabinet with drawers, some very shallow, others up to four inches deep.

'In the shallow drawers he kept his *netsuke* – little toggles from Japanese traditional dress, most of 'em carved from ivory or wood or bone . . . '.

Words came from the major in short bursts with intervals as though a certain internal pressure had to build up before they could be discharged.

'Then there were the sword furnishings – mainly guards, and in the deeper drawers he kept his collection

26

of *inro* – lacquered boxes which used to be worn on the girdle . . . '

Parkyn opened a couple of felt-lined drawers – now empty. 'There wasn't enough stuff to fill all the drawers so in one of them he kept his service revolver along with other odds and ends. Everything went . . . '

'The thief got in through the window?'

Parkyn was mocking. 'As we found the window open and a pane of glass missing that seems probable.'

'At night?'

'Evening. I was out; my sister was in her room with the radio on.'

'This was shortly after your father's death?'

'Two or three months, I suppose. The stuff had been valued for probate along with everything else.'

The door opened and a tall, grey, bony woman came in to stand just inside the door. The family resemblance was unmistakable, even to the lustreless, slightly bulging eyes.

'What is it, Gavin? What are you doing in father's room?' Her manner was that of an irritable parent to a child.

Parkyn took his sister's arrival and her revealing question in his stride. 'My sister: Chief Superintendent Wycliffe and Sergeant Kersey . . . ' He added, 'The superintendent found father's gun on the beach at St Juliot and he thinks it had been recently fired.'

'Indeed!' Unimpressed. 'I do not like people in this room.'

Wycliffe said, 'I intend to re-open the inquiry into the theft. I can't hold out much hope but we shall do our best. Your brother has been good enough to answer a few questions.'

'Questions! We had enough questions last time with no result.'

Hetty was a few years older than her brother; her grey

hair was thin and wispy, her skin dry and wrinkled and whatever reserves of human warmth and emotion she may have had seemed to have seeped away with her femininity.

'How well known was your father's collection?'

Parkyn said, 'He built it up over a great number of years mainly through his contacts in Japan though occasionally he bought through London salerooms . . . He corresponded with a few collectors but I doubt if many people knew of the collection.'

Hetty spoke as though her brother had not opened his mouth. 'I think it must have been very well known. The man who came to value it for probate said that it was a celebrated collection – those were his words – "a celebrated collection".' Dogmatic emphasis.

'Who was that?'

It was Parkyn who answered. 'A chap called Clement . . . The younger of two brothers who run an antique business in Bear Street. He's a specialist in that sort of thing.'

'I suppose there is an inventory or catalogue giving technical descriptions of the items in the collection?'

Kersey said, 'There was one in the file of the case, sir.'

'Then we can circulate the dealers. By this time the chances are that a few of the things may have found their way back into the legitimate market and we may be able to get a lead from there.'

Parkyn came with them down the garden to where the car was parked. They stood for a moment by the car. Wycliffe said, 'You realize that I am most concerned about the gun.'

Once more he had the impression that the major was faintly amused. He said, 'I wish you luck, Superintendent . . . And good-day.'

As Wycliffe was being driven away he looked back at the major, standing on the pavement, motionless. It was hard to imagine the life he and his sister must lead in that gloomy house. Did they ever carry on a normal conversation? Did they ever laugh together? Or even quarrel?

Wycliffe said, 'Didn't you say something about Parkyn calling each morning at the antique shop?'

'Yes, I did, sir. He seems quite matey with the elder brother, not the one who did the valuation.' Kersey broke off while he negotiated the awkward double twist which gave the lane its name. 'At the time I had an idea along those lines but I got rapped for it.'

'What lines?' .

'Well, as I understand it, the major didn't figure in his father's will; everything went to the delectable Hetty. God knows why.'

'So?'

'About the time of his father's death he sold his boat which he'd kept at St Juliot for a couple of years before that. Backing horses – especially his sort – can be an expensive pastime.'

'So you thought he might have engineered the break-in with the help of his friends in the antique shop?'

'It occurred to me as a possibility but the notion wasn't popular with my D.I. at the time and I got rapped for slanting the inquiry in that direction.'

'Why?'

'I've no idea, sir.'

'Are the Clement brothers crooks, in your opinion?'

'I've no reason to think so, it just seemed to me a line worth following up.'

As they reached the bottom of the lane where it joined Bear Street, Kersey said, 'Where to, sir?'

'Drop me at home.'

In Bear Street Kersey slowed almost to a stop as they passed the antique shop. The frontage dated from before the first war and the paintwork was neglected and peeling. The shop was double-fronted with tall narrow panes of glass, arched at the top, and the fascia was decorated with elaborate cast-iron ornament. In one of the windows a card on an easel read: 'We buy and sell fine antiques of every description and we are specialists in oriental *objets d'art*. Collections purchased. Qualified valuers.'

'So you're here.'

'Sorry I couldn't let you know.'

Helen was making a white sauce. In the living-room a record player made sweet music.

'Recognize it?'

He listened and thought furiously. He was being tested as part of his musical education. 'It's one of the Mahler symphonies.'

'Good! Which?'

'Well, we've only got four of them and it's not the one with the soprano soloist – I'll say it's number six.'

'Wrong! It is the one with the soprano soloist – number four.'

'Anyway, I'm improving. What's for lunch?'

'Chicken casserole. I thought if you didn't come home I could put it in the oven again this evening.' She poured the sauce into a sauce-boat.

'What's all this about a gun?'

'I found it on the beach by the quay – loaded and recently fired. I've found since that it belonged to the late Lieutenant-General Sir Gavin Lloyd Parkyn, if that means anything to you.'

'Hetty's father.'

Wycliffe was impressed. 'You know them?'

Helen was full of surprises; she was not one of those women who exhaust themselves and their families with good works, neither was she a member of the coffee-morning fraternity, but her contacts, such as they were, seemed to provide her with a great deal of information about life in the city at all levels.

'I don't know them but Joan Langford who comes to the art classes lives next door to them in Garrison Drive.

Hetty is something of a cross; she's taken a dislike to Joan and she shows it by dumping her more unpleasant garbage over the hedge. When Joan complains she says it must be the sea-gulls.'

'What about Hetty's brother? What does she say about him?'

'Very little except that he must have a lot to put up with. Do you have to go out again?'

'I'm afraid so.'

After lunch he drove to headquarters in his own car – a Rover, chosen not because he knew anything about the relative merits of cars but because it was British and he refused to 'go foreign' even if the thing broke down twice a month – which it didn't.

Dixon, one of the young hopefuls he had let loose at St Juliot, was in the duty room typing his report.

'We didn't find anything, sir. Two of the cottagers reckoned they'd heard a car in the small hours. A Mrs Clara Barton—'

'From the corner house?'

'That's right. She says she was woken by a car engine whining, then it was quiet for a moment, after that the car seemed to drive off normally.'

'I suppose she heard the car being reversed off the jetty.'

'That's what I thought and so did she. She says couples sometimes spend half the night down there but they don't usually drive out on to the quay.' Dixon paused. 'I questioned her husband but he hadn't heard anything. Sleeping it off, by the look of him.'

'That's more than likely.'

'A Mrs Pascoe from the third cottage tells the same story except that she heard a shout which seemed to come from the beach not long before she heard the car. She didn't take a lot of notice because some of the local lads often go out for a night's fishing on Saturdays if the tide is right.'

'Was anybody out last night?'

'Yes, sir. Two brothers – Nicky and Charlie Byrd, but we haven't seem them yet. By the time we heard about them they'd gone off to town and they're not expected back until the pubs shut.'

Dixon glanced at his notes. 'We measured the tracks and took a few photographs and I've sent the results to the Vehicle Department for their opinion.'

Wycliffe had the file concerned with the original break-in sent up from the basement and sat at his desk turning over the papers which were neatly clipped together in sets. The work had been done thoroughly and as far as he could see there was no line of inquiry which had not been followed up.

In bed that night, in the small hours when self-criticism is at its most coldly clinical and its probes are sharpest, he concluded that he was making a fool of himself over a gun; building up a case out of nothing more than unlawful possession and disposal.

CHAPTER TWO

Monday. Another fine day. The sun had come round to shine through the window of Wycliffe's office revealing smears on his desk-top and dust on his bookcase. It was the weather to start thinking of holidays, not the two or three weeks of expensive frustration in some strange place, but the holiday idea – the holiday ideal.

His personal assistant, Diane, came in, smelling of eau-de-Cologne, immaculate, efficient and off-putting. His younger colleagues, frustrated in their licentious desires, called her the Ice Maiden. Maiden she certainly was. She brought a bundle of memoranda slips – bits of different coloured papers, the colours denoting their department of origin. Wycliffe recalled and regretted the days when, if you had something to say to some-body, you walked down the corridor, kicked open his door and said it. Now multi-coloured flimsies descended like leaves in autumn and because people had to write down their messages they said more and meant less.

'Put them there, Diane.'

She arranged the bits of paper in neat rows. One of them (pink for Vehicles) was headed, *Report on the Wheel Tracks at St Juliot Quay.* It made a typescript page out of the fact that an expert believed the tracks to be those of a B.L. Maxi but wasn't sure.

Kersey rang to say that Dixon had spoken to the Byrd brothers about their fishing trip. 'They arrived back at their moorings at about half-past two on Sunday morning and they saw a car reversing off the quay. They didn't take a lot of notice and I gather they were pretty far gone;

these trips seem to be more for boozing than fishing.'
Kersey paused, then went on, 'I wondered if you'd
thought any more about the Clement Brothers, sir?'

Kersey was dogged. Wycliffe had thought about them
and decided that grounds for connecting them with the
robbery and the gun were too slender. Was it likely that
a local dealer, an accredited valuer, would connive with
a householder in theft? He thought not. In any case he
couldn't see Major Parkyn as the other party. But when
Diane's appetite for paperwork was finally satisified he
said, 'I'm going down to Bear Street, if anybody wants
me they can try the car radio.'

He collected his car from the park and drove through
the heavy morning traffic. He was not a good driver; he
enjoyed no rapport with the internal combustion
engine nor, indeed, with the age which had deified it.
He often told himself that he had been born out of due
time, that he should have muscled in on the age of steam
and grown old while, among other things, it was still
possible to be a Fabian Socialist and believe in the
perfectibility of man.

He left his car in front of the old custom-house which
brought back memories of another case* and entered
Bear Street from that end. In the morning sunshine it
looked like a street scene by Pissarro; the light seemed
to vibrate, softening outlines, dazzling the eyes. It was all
a great deal more animated than it had been on Sunday
morning. The street was noted for its specialist shops: a
high-class grocery, a well-stocked delicatessen, a good
wine shop, a home bakery and a discriminating butcher
. . . Young and middle-aged women, golf-club wives,
subscribers to *House and Garden*, parked their Mini
Metros, their Fiats and their Fiestas and worked their
systematic ways through the street with exotic shopping
lists. In all this the neglected paintwork and murky

* Death in Stanley Street

windows of the antique shop stood out like a poor relation at a wedding.

Wycliffe spotted Parkyn some way ahead; he still wore his sailor's jersey and corduroys, but with canvas shoes, and he carried a string bag full of groceries. At the antique shop he paused and peered in, shielding his eyes from the light with one hand; then he was on his way again, covering the ground rapidly with his curious gait which seemed to involve scarcely any movement of the body above the knees. He glided as though on wheels.

The antique shop was closed. Wycliffe rang the side-door bell but there was no reply. He was aware of being watched by a woman in the café-restaurant opposite. The morning coffee trade was over and lunch had not yet started so she had no customers. He crossed the street and sat at one of the tables which was covered with a red and white checked cloth. The woman was fat with almost black hair and attractive amiable features; she spoke in a soft Devonshire brogue, rich and thick as clotted cream.

'Coffee?'

'Black, please.'

She went to the coffee machine.

'I can't get any answer opposite.'

'No, they're closed.' She moved slowly, shifting her weight from one foot to the other with deliberation. She was eyeing him, sizing him up in a way that all policemen know well.

'Police?'

'Yes.'

'I thought so. What's happening over there?'

'Nothing that I know of.'

She was looking across at the shop with a thoughtful air. 'There's something, and I'm a bit worried.' She twisted a gold wedding ring on her finger. 'They're a couple of bachelors. Joseph, the elder brother, comes in

35

here most days for his mid-day meal, and David comes sometimes when he's home. The shop was open as usual on Saturday and Joseph was in at lunch-time. Sunday, I didn't see them all day and they didn't draw back the curtains in their sitting-room; this morning, they haven't opened the shop. I said about it to my husband. Of course they're never very fussy about opening hours, they'll put up a notice, "Back in ten minutes" and stay away all morning . . . All the same . . . '

'Don't they sometimes go away together?'

'Never. Joseph never goes away and David is away at least half his time.'

She moved back to her customary place behind the counter. An appetising smell came from the kitchen and it seemed a good idea to lunch there.

'Your husband does the cooking?'

She nodded. 'Do you like pot roast?'

'It smells good.'

She laughed, a rich attractive laugh. 'We cater mainly for regulars at lunch times but if you want to stay . . . '

A girl in a blue trouser-suit came down the street on the opposite side. She had dark shoulder-length hair and a good figure but her features were a little too sharp. She tried the door of the antique shop, rattled it, then tried the side-door and ended up by ringing the bell, keeping her finger on the button for some time.

'There you are! If they'd gone away or anything, she would know.'

'Who is she?'

'She's called Stokes and she's David's girl-friend.'

'She looks young.'

'I don't know about that; she must be twenty-four or five.'

It dawned on him that he was assuming the Clement brothers to be at least middle-aged; two ageing bachelors cultivating their grey hairs and their paunches and indulging their whims. 'So they're young men?'

36

'Don't you know them?'

'We've never met.'

She considered, pouting her lips like a schoolgirl with a problem. 'They're not exactly young. Joseph must be in the middle forties and David is thirty-one or two. They're not a bit alike. Joseph is stocky like his father and a red-head; David is slight and very dark, like his mother. Joseph took over the business when his father died. He lost both of them – mother and father, inside a fortnight – influenza followed by pneumonia.' She sighed. 'That must be ten or twelve years ago.

'Ever since then Joseph has taken his mid-day meal here. Of course, David has only been in the business about three years. I remember him as a schoolboy, then he went away to college and after that he got a job in London with a big insurance company. We didn't see much of him for years; then, apparently, he got tired of life in London, chucked up his job and came back here.'

'Do the two brothers get on together?'

She hesitated. 'They seem to but I'm not sure. David does a lot of travelling and they say he's got the right connections among collectors and such like. It suits him to be always on the move, just as it suits Joseph to be a stay-at-home. All the same, I've had a feeling lately that Joseph isn't happy with the way things are going.'

The restaurant began to fill and the fat woman was kept going, to and fro between the hatch and the tables. Although she moved with such deliberation and never allowed herself to be hurried, she kept pace with the orders and found time to exchange gossip and wise-cracks with her customers.

'Do you want a drink?'

'I'd like a lager with this.'

The pot roast was delicious but not the sort of meal to go back to work on. The lunch-time customers included a surprising number of young people from neighbouring offices but some of them were content with a bowl of soup and a bread-roll. From time to time a little man in a chef's hat supported on his ears, looked in; he stood in the doorway of the kitchen and exchanged greetings with the customers in English that was resourceful if inaccurate.

The fat woman smiled affectionately. 'Czech, from Prague. He came over in the '68 uprising.'

Wycliffe kept an eye on the antique shop. One or two people stopped to look in the window but nobody tried to enter the shop and nobody rang the bell.

He left the restaurant after his meal and walked down the street on the same side as the antique shop until he came to a narrow alley, a mere passage between two shops. It led to a back lane where grass grew through the cracks in the tarmacadam. Each of the buildings on that side of Bear Street had a backyard and a door opening into the lane. The Clement brothers had a garage as well. The yard door opened easily.

The yard, paved with moss-covered bricks, was scarcely big enough to turn round in. There was no car in the garage. Two ground-floor windows faced the yard, they had not been opened in years and were covered with a wire-mesh, but through one of them he could see the glow of a lamp – a desk or table lamp to judge from the level. The house door was solid and there was no bell or knocker but to his surprise, when he put his hand to the knob, it opened easily. He rapped on it with his knuckles and when this brought no response he pushed it wide and called out. No-one came so he went in. The room, previously the kitchen of the house, was now a cloakroom with a washbasin and a cubicle housing a W.C. To his right was another door which led into the room from which the light came.

It was an office with a large desk, a swivel chair, a filing cabinet and a massive, old-fashioned safe, painted black, with brass fittings. On the desk was a telephone and an adjustable lamp which was switched on; a sale catalogue lay open on the blotter, a ball-point pen beside it. There was a perpetual calendar and an ashtray almost full of stubs and an empty cigarette pack. Wycliffe's first impression was that someone had just slipped out. Except that the room had a chilly, unused feel and the calendar, for what it was worth, showed Saturday 9th instead of Monday 11th.

He crossed the room to another door which led to the shop, a dimly lit cavern with a musty resinous smell. At the back of the shop, screened from the street by the furniture display, there were tables and a showcase laid out with porcelain and glass, a few bits of ivory and silver and a collection of coins. Apart from a monumental lacquered cabinet there was nothing to suggest an interest in oriental antiques.

In one corner an iron spiral staircase led to the floor above. He climbed the steps and came to a landing from which conventional stairs went down to the side-door and a corridor led off to the first-floor rooms.

'Is anybody home?'

He pushed open the first door he came to; a sitting room. A conventional three-piece, the worse for wear; a television set, a moth-eaten carpet ... The window overlooked Bear Street and the restaurant opposite. The next room along the passage was a bedroom with a double bed, wardrobe and chest-of-drawers, Edwardian style. On a bedside table there was a studio photograph of the girl in the blue trouser-suit. She was pretty but her sharp features, rather pinched, suggested the acute aggressive awareness of certain small animals.

On the other side of the passage, at the back of the house, there was a kitchen and bathroom which had been modern fifty years ago, then a room furnished as a bed-sitter. There was a desk placed under the window and it was a moment before he saw the body of a man lying on the floor by the desk, a man with red hair.

He bent over the man; he was dead, shot through the

right side of the skull, behind the ear. Round the wound of entry he thought he could see the faint impression of a gun muzzle. The body lay in a twisted position, the left side of the face in contact with the floor, obscuring the exit wound which must have been extensive to judge from the blood and tissue on the carpet.

Suicide? No sign of the gun but it could be hidden under the body. Murder was a possibility.

The man had been working on his stamp collection; there was a loose-leaf album on the desk, a few stamps in polythene envelopes, a magnifier and a pair of forceps. There was a pipe too, and other pipes in a rack on the wall by the desk, an ashtray and a tobacco jar.

Shelves over a single bed held books about stamps, catalogues, albums, and a collection of works on English furniture. Wycliffe liked the look of it all; he had a soft spot for collectors, most of whom were amiable even when slightly dotty.

He left the room and went down the spiral staircase which vibrated with his every step. Back in the office behind the shop he telephoned headquarters and spoke to Kersey.

The gun on the beach had led him to this but was there really a link? He would only know when the bullet which killed the red-head had been found and a comparison test made by a ballistics expert.

While waiting for his men he looked over the things on the desk. The catalogue referred to a London auction, held several months earlier, and it was open at a page which listed a collection of glass paperweights. A sum of money had been pencilled against each item – presumably the price fetched at auction, and the amounts varied from three hundred to well over three thousand pounds. Six of the more costly weights had heavily scored lines against them in the margin of the page.

Standing between the desk and the safe he noticed for

the first time a broken statuette, it was a Parian figure of a nude girl and it looked as though it might have been knocked off the desk. A struggle? If so, there seemed to be no other signs.

Kersey was the first to arrive. Wycliffe had told them to use the back lane to avoid turning their activities into a spectator sport. Kersey had an I-told-you-so look. 'Dr Franks was at the hospital – some committee meeting – but they've been in touch and he's on his way.'

Franks was the pathologist.

'Who's dead?'

'Presumably the eldest brother, Joseph, I gather he was a red-head.'

'Murder?'

'I'm going to treat it as murder for the moment but it could turn out to be suicide?'

'How did he die?'

'Shot but there was no gun to be seen. It could be under the body.'

'Or it could be with old Melville at Ballistics.'

No need to answer that.

'Did either of the Clement brothers have a car?'

'David, the younger one, did – a blue Maxi, I think.'

'It's not in the garage and David doesn't seem to be around.'

Smith arrived with two more detectives but until the pathologist had examined the body there was little they could do. Wycliffe left them in the office and went upstairs to get the feel of the place. As before he was struck by its threadbare shabbiness. Two bachelors, neither of them houseproud; tobacco-ash in saucers, mouldy scraps of food forgotten in kitchen cupboards, grubby linen and a faint but pervasive smell of sweaty socks. He started in the sitting-room. Apart from the worn and dusty suite there was a bookcase with books mostly on antiques, and on the floor, stacks of trade journals and sale catalogues in no sort of order. The pictures on the walls were dreary over-varnished land-scapes which looked as though they had failed to draw a bid at some sale. Apart from them there was a framed photograph, presumably of the brothers, taken years ago.

The one Wycliffe identified as Joseph was a stocky young man in his twenties; he looked at the camera with a dutiful if tentative smile on his heavy face. His brother, a schoolboy, had made no such concession, his expression was one of bored indifference. He was cast in a different mould from his brother, a thin, intelligent face and a look which, despite the disparity in their ages, suggested that it was he rather than Joseph who had sized up the business of living and come to terms with it.

The spiral staircase vibrated under at least two pairs of feet and Wycliffe heard Franks in the passage. It would not be long now. After a few minutes he went out into the passage and joined Smith who was taking photographs from the doorway of the dead man's room as the pathologist turned the body over for examination. Franks glanced up and saw Wycliffe.

'Hullo, Charles! If this is suicide then somebody nicked the gun, it isn't here. He was shot through the temporal bone just above and slightly behind the mastoid process – an unusual spot for murder or suicide. *If* he shot himself he may have read about bullets passing through the frontal lobes and not doing their job. It's surprising the things people know these days. When I started in the business not many knew their palate from their patella. I suppose they learn in the hope of defending themselves against bloody doctors . . . The wound of exit is a fair sized hole as you probably gathered from the mess on the carpet. The left side of the skull is completely shattered. I'd guess the bullet lost most of its momentum and is probably lying on the floor somewhere.'

Franks dribbled a continuous flow of words. He

reminded one of a baby, pink, bald and shining. He shifted the body to a fresh position and Smith's camera clicked again.

'Seems he was keen on stamps. People with a hobby don't often do themselves in unless things get badly screwed up.' He straightened, brushing the knees of his trousers, and turned to Wycliffe. 'Well, you can have him shifted when you like – give your chaps a chance to start work.'

'Time of death?'

Franks passed a plump hand over his bald head. 'He's been dead quite a while.'

'How would Saturday night fit? Say, sometime between the shop closing and Sunday morning?'

Franks considered. 'Forty-odd hours. That might do. Look at the extruded muck – the way its's congealed. Anyway, I'll do what I can and ring later.'

Two men carried the body away on a stretcher. There was no question of taking it down the spiral staircase and so it had to go by way of the side-door and out into Bear Street where it attracted plenty of attention.

The body gone, Franks looked round the little room. 'Perhaps you'll get someone to send me that little square of carpet – it will have to be cut out. Who's attending?'

A police officer attends a post-mortem whenever it is likely that a court case will follow.

Wycliffe said, 'Scales will be here directly, I'll send him along.'

With the body and the pathologist out of the way work could begin.

Clement must have been sitting at his desk when he was shot (or shot himself). His body had slipped between desk and chair, pushing the chair aside as he collapsed to the floor. If he had been bending over his stamps and someone had come into the room he might not have looked up. Absorbed in his work he could have acknowledged the visitor with a muttered word. A

43

moment later he would have felt the cold contact of the gun against his skin then the fleeting but final trauma before oblivion.

That would account for the unusual position of the wound of entry and it would be murder. Wycliffe tried to convince himself. Why would anyone remove the weapon from the scene of a suicide? And the weapon itself? Surely Joseph must have been shot by the gun on the beach, one chamber fired, wiped clean of prints? But if so, why had it been ditched, and ditched so ineffectually at St Juliot?

Guessing games. But one thing seemed certain, his idea that a body had been disposed of at the quay was a non-starter.

John Scales, his deputy, arrived and Wycliffe sent him to join Franks at the post-mortem. Three more men turned up from headquarters, drafted to the new case as they reported back from other jobs. He briefed them.

'House-to-house in Bear Street and the immediate neighbourhood. Get a move on before the shops shut. Get what you can on the Clement brothers and don't turn your noses up at gossip. The critical period seems to have been from the time the shops closed on Saturday until the small hours of Sunday morning. The younger brother is missing; so is his car – probably a blue Maxi but get details from Vehicle Records and have them circulated.'

He followed the men out into the back lane where a constable in a patrol car was maintaining radio watch and gave instructions for an incident caravan to be parked in front of the old custom-house by the harbour. These vans are self-contained incident posts with radio-telephone links and accommodation for limited office work and interviews. A handy base for men working on the case and somewhere convenient for locals to go with information if they have any.

Back in the house Joseph Clement's room was being systematically and minutely investigated.

The sight of large men moving about a small room, solemnly and ponderously circumspect, engaged in the most zany tasks, always struck Wycliffe as bizarre and slightly ludicrous. Dixon was on his knees cutting out the square of carpet where Joseph's head had rested; the middle-aged D.C. Fowler was crawling about, examining the floor inch by inch in search of the missing bullet; Sergeant Smith was testing likely surfaces for prints and pausing now and then to photograph what he found.

A room is immortalized by having someone killed in it. The most prosaic little room has only to become the scene of a murder to be dissected, studied and recorded with at least as much skill and care as would be expended on an important archaeological site. The anatomy of the room goes on file in the form of inventories, plans and photographs, which are preserved with as much care as the site records of an Arthur Evans or a Mortimer Wheeler.

He left them to it and crossed the street to the restaurant where he had lunched. It was closed, but there was a card in the window saying that it would reopen at seven for dinner. He tapped on the glass door and after a moment or two the fat woman came through from the back premises. She recognized him and opened the door.

'I thought you might be back.'

'The girl in the blue trouser-suit – Stokes, I think you said – do you know where she lives?'

'I saw them coming out with a stretcher; who was it?'

'Joseph.'

Her eyes glistened on the verge of tears. 'I was afraid so. Poor man! He never did anybody any harm. How did it happen?'

45

'He died of a bullet wound but that's all I know at the moment. About this girl . . . '

'She lives in Godolphin Street, just round the corner. It's a house which has been converted into flats; I think it's number 15 but you can't miss it.'

'Thanks.'

'I don't know if you'll find her home; she's a nurse at the Horton Radford so it depends what shift she's on.'

The Horton Radford was a private hospital, expensive and exclusive.

'What about David?' The fat woman wanted as much as possible.

'I haven't seen him; that's why I want to talk to the girl.'

It was four o'clock and the children were going home from a nearby junior school. The sky had clouded over and great drops of rain made circular patches on the pavements. It looked like the start of a thunder shower but Godolphin Street was not so far.

Number 15 was a Georgian town house which had been converted into flats while preserving the frontage. Once inside there was little evidence of Georgian elegance. The name board gave M.K. Stokes as the occupant of flat three on the first floor. Wycliffe climbed the stairs and rang the door-bell.

He had almost given up when the door was opened on a chain and he saw the face of the girl in the trouser-suit but her eyes were puffy and her hair was confined in a net. He showed her his warrant card.

She hesitated but did not ask what he wanted. 'Wait a minute.'

The door was closed again but after a full two minutes she opened it wide. 'You'd better come in.'

She had run a comb through her hair and put on a dressing-gown. Perhaps she had used cleansing tissues for her skin looked less shiny.

The room was small, just big enough for a couple of

armchairs, a table, a bookcase and a televison set. The tall, rectangular window with its many panes, part of the original house, seemed incongruous. The place had a woman's smell, a woman who was not fastidious.

'I was in bed; I'm a nurse at the Horton Radford and I'm on nights.' She lit a cigarette and drew on it with the single-minded concentration of an addict, then she perched herself on the arm of one of the chairs and drew her dressing-gown about her legs; her feet were bare. She looked at him and her manner was more speculative than apprehensive. 'Is it about David Clement?'

'Why do you ask that?'

'David Clement at the antique shop – I'm beginning to be a bit worried. I haven't heard from him since Saturday and now the shop is shut.'

Wycliffe was stolidly unforthcoming. 'I want to get in touch with the Clement brothers and I thought you might be able to help.'

'Has something happened?'

'It's possible that there has been a break-in at the shop; the back door was unsecured and we've no way of knowing whether there has been an intruder on the premises until we get in touch with one of the brothers.'

She seemed to accept this. 'I don't know where they are; I can't understand it. David and I had a loose arrangement for Sunday morning but he didn't show up. I rang the shop a couple of times but there was no answer and this morning they were shut.' She swept her hair back from her eyes in a nervous gesture. 'David is pretty casual and it wouldn't be the first time he's gone off somewhere without letting me know but Joseph should be there.'

She had the professional self-assurance of most nurses and she had cultivated a manner of speech appropriate to the Horton Radford where patients arrived and left in chauffeur-driven limousines but neither was more than skin-deep and underneath she was probably a very ordinary young woman.

'Were you expecting bad news?'

'No – not at all!' She crossed her legs in a vigorous movement. 'I'm a bit bothered, that's all. It's natural, isn't it?'

The room had two doors apart from the one by which he had come in; one stood open to the kitchen in which it would hardly have been possible to take more than a couple of steps, the other was shut and led, presumably, to the bedroom.

'How well do you know him?'

'Well enough but what's that got to do with it?' She paused then went on, 'We've been seeing each other for more than a year and sleeping together when the occasion offered. Will that do?'

He told her about Joseph and she was clearly shocked. 'You mean that Joseph is dead – murdered?'

'It looks like murder but in any case it's important to get hold of his brother.'

She hesitated as though trying to come to grips with what she had heard. 'You're not suggesting that David killed him?'

Wycliffe was non-committal. 'I've told you all I know; Joseph is dead and David is missing.'

She looked at him, trying to make up her mind. 'I hope you're being straight with me because you can forget the idea of David killing his brother or anybody else.'

'You seem very sure.'

'I am. Like a lot of small men David can be aggressive but there's no violence in him. When you've slept with a man you know these things.' She stood up with nervous vigour and crushed out her cigarette in an ashtray on the mantelpiece. 'What do you want from me?'

'Information. When did you last see David?'

He had to wait while she lit another cigarette, fumbling

48

with her lighter. 'Saturday evening. As a matter of fact, Saturday was my day off and we spent the afternoon together until half-past seven or a bit later. He left then because he had an appointment at the shop.'

'Did he say who the appointment was with?'

From the sudden change in her expression it was obvious that an idea had occurred to her but all she said was, 'No, just that it was some chap who wanted to sell something. It was nothing unusual; a lot of their business is done after hours – buying and selling.'

'When you were with him on Saturday did he seem his usual self?'

'Quite!' She frowned as though trying to recollect the day. 'He came over just after lunch and we drove out to Hembury where an old girl had some family heirlooms she wanted to sell. They were mainly bits of silver and not of much account so David wasn't interested. We came back here, I cooked a meal, and sometime before eight he left.'

'And you haven't heard from him or seen him since?'

'No, I told you. We had a tentative date for Sunday morning – I was half expecting him to come over for me but he didn't turn up.'

'How did the brothers get on?'

'All right, I think; probably better than most brothers who work in the same business. Joe is – was a good deal older and a bit of a drag where anything new was concerned but David usually managed to edge him along without having rows.'

'Did Joseph have a woman friend?'

She laughed. 'I shouldn't think so; women scared him.'

'Did he go out much?'

'I don't know. If I went to the flat of an evening he was sometimes there, sometimes not. It didn't make any difference, if he was there he would be shut up in his room with his precious stamps.'

'Is the business prosperous?'

'I suppose so. David never seems to be short.'

'Have they any relatives?'

'Their parents are both dead, I do know that. As to aunts, uncles and the rest I've no idea. I've never heard David speak of any.'

Her room gave little away; it was as impersonal as a room in a boarding house. No pictures, no photographs, no books; just one or two ornaments which could have come from a fairground.

'When David was here on Saturday, did he have his car?'

'No, we went to Hembury in my Mini; I like driving.'

'Have they got many friends?'

'I shouldn't think so. David doesn't make friends easily and Joe ... I suppose Joe must go out with somebody when he isn't home but I've no idea who.'

'Major Parkyn?'

She grinned. 'Popeye! Could be, I suppose.'

Wycliffe was asking questions at random – fishing, and prepared for anything he might catch. There was something odd about the girl's attitude but he couldn't put his finger on it. She was surprised and shocked by Joseph's death and concerned about her boy-friend but . . .

'Do you think they had any enemies?'

'Enemies? I shouldn't think so, they weren't the sort to go around upsetting people.'

Rain beat against the window and he could glimpse a leaden sky above the houses opposite.

'Have you a photograph of David?'

'A photograph? Not a proper one; I've probably got a few snapshots.' She looked at him accusingly. 'You *do* think he shot Joe!'

'I think nothing of the sort but if he really is missing then we have to find him.'

She got up and went into the bedroom to return in a few minutes with three snapshots. 'That's the best I can do.'

One of them showed David Clement in swimming trunks on the foredeck of a cabin cruiser and the girl, in a bikini, at his side. She had her hand on his shoulder and she was an inch or two taller.

'Who does the boat belong to?'

'To David.'

'You didn't tell me he had a boat.'

'You didn't ask me.'

'Where does he keep it?'

'At the moment it's moored off St Juliot but all winter she's been laid up in Morcom's yard.'

'When did he put her off to moorings?'

She frowned. 'A week or ten days ago. He's keen on cruising and he likes to make the season last as long as possible.'

'Is it a big boat?'

'Depends what you call big; she's got a four berth cabin and the usual offices.'

'What's she called?'

'He re-christened her *Manna* when he bought her. It was a joke because he bought her with an unexpected windfall.'

This opened up possibilities which looked bad for David Clement. Wycliffe put the photographs in his pocket. 'I'll take these and I'd like a brief description of him.'

'If you must. He's about five-feet-five, thin, with almost black hair and rather pale skin . . . '

'What was he wearing when you last saw him?'

'A fawn denim bush-jacket and slacks with fawn suede shoes. I think he had on a sort of grey-green shirt.'

Wycliffe stared at the girl with dreamy eyes, wondering how much she knew that she was not prepared to say; a profitless speculation.

'In the office behind the shop there's a little Parian figure of a naked girl lying, smashed, on the floor.'

'Smashed?' She looked surprised. 'That's Monica.

David kept her on the desk to tease Joseph who's very straight-laced. Actually Monica is a bit naughty. David says she's one of a set of six designs made by a Victorian potter for a rich customer to give as presents to his friends . . . Joseph wasn't killed in the office, was he?'

'No, in his room.'

It seemed that there was nothing to be gained by staying so he left. Outside the streets were wet but it had stopped raining; thunder rumbled around with the occasional flash of lightning. He felt like a juggler who is trying to keep too many balls in the air at once; more accurately, like someone trying to make a jig-saw puzzle with pieces which don't all belong. The revolver on the beach, the break-in at Parkyn's, Joseph's body in his room, the Saturday-night caller at the shop, the open door of the house, the light left burning, David's disappearance, the car, the boat . . .

David had left the flat in Godolphin Street before eight on Saturday night to keep an appointment with his client, an appointment which might or might not have involved Joseph. Now Joseph was dead and David had disappeared. A car had been heard and seen on the quay at St Juliot early on Sunday morning and Parkyn's revolver had been dropped on the beach at about the same time.

The boat added a new dimension and it was almost certainly the link between St Juliot and the rest.

A police Range Rover was edging its way along Bear Street with one of the blue incident vans in tow. News of trouble at the antique shop had spread and a single uniformed copper was having his work cut out keeping people on the move.

A reporter from one local paper recognized Wycliffe. 'What's happened to the other brother, Mr Wycliffe?'

He said, 'We are trying to make contact,' and escaped into the shop. He found Kersey in the office at the back. 'How are they getting on?'

'Dixon has finished his bit of carpet surgery and the piece has gone to Franks. Fowler found the bullet under Joseph's bed in a pile of fluff which must have been there since Adam; I've sent it to Melville. It's a bit flattened but I've seen worse used in comparison tests. Smith is still working on the bedroom and the others are going over the rest of the flat.'

'You haven't touched anything down here?'

'Not yet.'

'Good! The Clements had a client due at eight on Saturday evening. He wanted to sell something and the chances are they did their business here. When Smith has finished upstairs he'd better start on this.'

'Anything else?'

'Yes; observation on Molly Stokes. She lives in a flat round the corner in Godolphin Street. Twenty-four hour obo but no interference. She's a nurse at the Horton Radford and I want her tailed going and coming. It's important she shouldn't know she's being watched . . . Oh, yes, if possible I'd like a photograph of her in her street clothes.'

'David's girl-friend?' Kersey's ugly, intelligent face was alive with curiosity.

'Yes, I had the impression that while she was shocked to hear of Joseph's death, her boy-friend's disappearance was less of a surprise. I'm not saying she expected it, only that she didn't seem as concerned as she might have been.'

'You think she knows where he is?'

'It's possible. Anyway, it's worth keeping an eye on her for a day or two.'

He went back through the shop and up the spiral staircase. Dixon and Fowler were working in the sitting room, searching and sorting with the curtains drawn and the lights on though it was still daylight outside. What they were doing was probably a waste of time but one can never tell. Detection is a labour-intensive industry.

He looked in on Smith and handed over the snap-shots he had got from the girl. 'Suitable enlargements for circulation when you can.'

The wheels were beginning to turn.

He went downstairs and let himself out by the side-door. It was raining again and this had cleared the street more effectively than the lone policeman who was sheltering in a doorway. The fat woman in the restaurant was setting the tables for dinner. Each table now had an ornamental candlestick in the middle of the check cloth. He turned down Bear Street to the harbour where the incident van was in position outside the old custom-house. In the little duty-room a young detective constable was filing house-to-house reports and the silence was broken only by occasional exchanges on the police radio.

'Telephone working?'

'Yes, sir.'

He looked up a number and dialled.

'Mrs Williams? . . . Is Toby about?'

Toby Williams was a St Juliot man. Retired, he supplemented his pension by keeping an eye on the craft moored off the village. His garden ran down to the shore and he had a shed where owners kept some of their gear.

'Mr Wycliffe?' Toby's bellow vibrated in the receiver. 'Is it about that little craft you thought of buying? . . . *Manna*? Mr Clement's boat – Yes, I look after 'er but she ain't 'ere now; 'e took 'er off sometime Saturday night – anyways she was 'ere Saturday night and she was gone Sunday morning . . . No, I weren't worried because 'e left a note in my shed like they all do.'

Wycliffe said, 'I'll look in for a word on my way home if it's not too late. See if you can find that note.'

So *Manna* was missing. At least that made sense of the St Juliot angle. On the face of it David Clement had cleared off in his launch. After murdering his brother?

And what about his car? If he had driven himself to St Juliot alone, the car should still be there. But were there two men involved? Two men of whom one had gone off in the launch and the other in the car. And the gun – had there been a scuffle in which the gun had been dropped and lost? One of the witnesses had mentioned a shout which seemed to come from the beach.

He needed to know more about the Clement brothers. The men on house-to-house would come back with the usual mix of fact and fiction but aside from that he had only the Stokes girl and the major. The fact that Parkyn regularly called at the antique shop on his daily round must mean something.

CHAPTER THREE

It was dark by the time he set out for Garrison Drive to talk to Parkyn. He climbed the steep slope of Dog's Leg Lane and came out on to the glacis where a cold, moist, salty wind off the sea took him by surprise. It was very dark and no feature of the coast was discernible except the clustered lights of Porthellin; the sea was a black void with a pin-point of light here and there marking the position of some ship. At precise intervals the beam of a distant lighthouse swept its arc across the sky. Three inadequate street lamps marked the line of the drive but all the houses seemed to be in darkness. He stumbled up the steep path of Number 3 and had to feel for the bell-push when he arrived at the front door. Having found it he kept his finger pressed and listened with satisfaction to a subdued but insistent buzzing somewhere in the house. Even so it was a long time before a light came on in the hall and he saw Hetty's gaunt form through the hammered glass panels of the door.

'Who is it?'

He was suddenly ashamed. If the woman was on her own in the house she had every right to be nervous in this lonely place.

'Superintendent Wycliffe.'

She seemed to hesitate and for a moment it was on the cards that she might turn back into the house and leave him standing, but finally she drew back two bolts and opened the door.

'Do you have to come at this time of night? Anyway, my brother is out.'

They were standing in the hall with a damp breeze blowing through the open door.

'May I come in and wait?'

'I've no idea how long he will be.'

He persisted; there was a chance he might learn something from Hetty though he was not optimistic. She gave in with a bad grace and he followed her down the passage to a little room between the drawing-room and the kitchen. It was furnished with a couple of armchairs, a bureau and a few bookshelves. An old oil-heater with a fretted top and a red window gave off a stuffy, smelly heat. An open book and a pair of glasses lay on one of the chairs.

Hetty's boudoir.

'You'd better sit down.'

He was still wearing his wet mackintosh and in a few minutes it would begin to steam. Hetty picked up her glasses and her book, sat down and resumed reading, holding the book high and close to her eyes. Of all things it was Vincent's *Defence of India*. The Parkyns were full of little surprises.

Hetty was well into her sixties, an age at which most women are grandmothers, aunts or both, and they have photographs on their walls to prove it. Hetty had her photographs but, as far as Wycliffe could tell, they were all of her father, the general. There were studio portraits of him in uniform at different ages and ranks but the greater number were of army occasions in which he was the central figure. Three, larger than the others and more elaborately framed, showed him in attendance on royalty and one of these bore an illustrious signature.

'I want to talk to your brother about the Clements.'

'What about them?' She did not look away from her book.

'Joseph, the elder brother, has been shot and David is missing.'

57

She turned her head. 'Indeed? I am sorry to hear it but how does it concern my brother?'

'I understand that he was a friend of the dead man.'

'Really? I know nothing of his friends.' And she resumed her reading as though there were no more to be said.

He had rarely met anyone so blankly unresponsive. Curiosity, nervousness, a desire for self-justification, even a simple dislike of silence, will usually prompt people to talk but now there was silence in the dreary little room without even the ticking of a clock to relieve it. Hetty must spend her evenings like this. Well, he had no justification for putting pressure on the woman and no desire to do so.

But after a while he became aware that she was eyeing him with quick, appraising glances. For a time it was almost a game between them. Evidently she was not as detached as she appeared; she wanted to say something but could not make up her mind. At last it came, dry and categorical.

'I see that you are interested in my photographs.'

He was non-committal. 'They seem to be an interesting record of your father's army career.'

'Only some of the highlights . . .' She looked at her book once more as though about to resume reading but it was obvious that having broken the ice she had more to say.

'We are an army family, Mr Wycliffe; my father, grandfather and great-grandfather on the Parkyn side were all generals and my mother came from a family with an army background.' She closed the book she had been reading and held it up with a bleak smile, 'I suppose my reading is not what you would expect of a woman . . .'

Probably Hetty had had few opportunities to talk to anyone since her father's death and here was a quiet, serious man who seemed to be receptive. What difference did it make that he was a policeman? She studied him, her prominent grey eyes intent and searching.

'It was natural that my father should want his only son to follow in the family tradition but Gavin was rather foolishly obstructive and difficult. Of course he was spoiled by my mother as a child. Anyhow, when father assumed that he would enter the army after Cambridge he deliberately enlisted in the navy.' She laughed without humour. 'But even they recognized that he was cut out for a soldier and persuaded him into the marines.'

Wycliffe listened with a bland expression on his face but said nothing.

'I am afraid my father and brother never *got on*.' Like Queen Victoria, Hetty had a habit of emphasizing certain words. She turned to look at the photographs of her father. 'He was a profoundly *religious* man in the tradition of many of our most distinguished generals. In his younger days they called him Pi-Parkyn but such cheap jibes never bothered him . . . '

Hetty's pale expressionless face was coming alive as though fresh blood had been injected into her veins. She launched with enthusiasm into a eulogy of the general in which he appeared as a bowdlerized version of Gordon, bible in one hand, sword of righteousness in the other and never a brandy bottle in sight.

Wycliffe listened with solemn attention and when she finished he said, 'Your father must have been a remarkable man.'

For the first time he saw her really smile. 'He was! A *most* remarkable man. As I have told you, he was a teetotaller and he hated – *hated* gambling.' She hesitated, then went on, lowering her voice, 'In that as in so many things, Gavin deliberately disregarded his wishes.' She paused, then added, 'And there were debts!'

She allowed time for her confidences to sink in.

'Of course, Gavin did well in the Korean affair.' Hetty

dismissed the whole Korean war as she might have done a frontier skirmish in the days of the Raj. 'It looked as though he was settling down and we were quite hopeful; then, shortly after the armistice in Korea, he allowed himself to be seconded to some quite absurd quasi-civilian appointment . . .' Her contempt was withering. 'It was a fresh blow to father's hopes for him and they drifted further and further apart . . . Then, when he finally came home for good, he adopted the extraordinay way of life which he now follows. I am *sure* that it contributed to father's death, *quite* sure.'

After a little while she added, 'So, as you see, my brother and I lead seperate lives.'

There was no answer to that so he said nothing.

'We have nothing in common and we have never been close. We live together only because it was my father's wish that I should provide a home for my brother.'

Another interval, then the final dénouement: 'You see, Mr Wycliffe, this is my house; father left everything to me.'

There was a sound from the back of the house, a door opened and closed and there were footsteps in the passage.

Hetty was alert. 'That will be my brother. If you want to talk to him hadn't you better go to him?'

'I assumed that he would come here.'

'Why should he?'

Why, indeed?

He found Parkyn in the dimly-lit hall taking off his duffle coat. The major greeted him with neither interest nor surprise. 'So you're here.' He hung up his wet coat on the hallstand and wiped his face and head with a red-spotted handkerchief. 'You'd better come to my room.' He pushed open the door of a room on the other side of the hall from his sister's. It was even more spartan; the carpet scarcely covered the floorboards. There was a

60

roll-topped desk, a table littered with old newspapers, and a couple of armchairs. A paraffin heater similar to Hetty's was already burning.

Long ago, as a child, Wycliffe had gone with his mother on some forgotten business, to visit their landlord, The Colonel, and been received by the great man in his study. That too had seemed, even to a little boy, untidy, dirty, and even smelly but when he had mentioned it to his mother afterwards she had said in a voice that was almost reverential, 'Those people are different, Charlie; not like us.' A line had been drawn which, in all the years since, he had found it difficult to cross. It accounted for his tentative attitude now.

'Pull up a chair and sit down.' Parkyn sat down himself and stretched his legs to the heater. 'I've just come from the antique shop. I rang the bell and a young copper answered it. "Who are you? What do you want? Answer at dictation speed so that I can write it in my bloody notebook" – sort of thing. Then he wouldn't tell me what it was all about.' Parkyn brought out his pipe and started to fill it. 'What's happened down there?'

'You've no idea?'

'If I had I wouldn't be asking.' He held out his pouch. 'Smoke?'

'Not just now.' Wycliffe told him what had happened and he listened without interruption.

'So Joseph is dead.'

'Yes. Was he a friend of yours?'

He gave Wycliffe a curious look. 'Friend? I've never thought about it.' He hesitated, choosing his words, 'He was a companion; we met fairly regularly. Joseph was a good fellow; one of nature's innocents. Good men often are – I expect you've noticed that in your job.' He glanced sideways at the superintendent. 'You haven't said that he was murdered but I suppose he was otherwise there wouldn't be all this flap.'

'We are treating it as a case of murder at the moment.'

So far, if this was an interrogation there was no doubt who was asking most of the questions.

Parkyn got up from his chair, went to his desk and returned with a bottle of whisky, two glasses and a carafe of rather murky looking water. 'Drink?'

'No, thanks.'

He glanced at Wycliffe with a half smile which could have been contemptuous, then he poured himself a drink, took a good swallow, wiped his lips and sighed. 'Of course you'll have no trouble catching him.'

'Who is it that we are supposed to catch?'

'The brother – David. You say his boat is missing but he won't get far; he's not very bright.'

Wycliffe stretched his legs to the heater and relaxed in his chair. He said, dryly, 'You seem rather better acquainted with the Clement brothers today than you were yesterday.'

Parkyn did not rise to that. He said, 'Indeed?' Then he added, as though making a simple statement of fact, 'David is a rat.'

He sipped his whisky then balanced the glass on the arm of his chair.

Wycliffe said, 'Perhaps you'd better tell me about your relationships with the brothers.'

'If you like, but there isn't much to tell—' He broke off as a board creaked in the passage and looked sharply towards the door, but after a moment he resumed speaking without lowering his voice. 'I've known Joseph for years, long before he made the mistake of letting his brother into the business. I see him a couple of times a week in the evening and I often call in at the shop in passing.'

'To collect his bets.'

'As you say.' No animosity, no embarrassment. The man was unassailable.

'And David?'

'I see as little of him as possible. It's not difficult to

avoid him as he seems to be away most of the time on his so-called business. I guessed a long time ago that he was lining his pocket at Joe's expense and that one day he would probably clear out and leave Joe stranded. Joe is no business man and lately, from things he's let drop, I'm sure that David has been disposing of stolen goods through the firm – what you people call fencing.'

Parkyn puffed at his pipe, sipped his whisky and sighed. 'Not that I would trouble myself about that but Joe's life centred on that shop and he was an honest man.'

'Has it occurred to you that the younger brother might have been involved in your break-in?'

Parkyn turned to face him briefly then looked away again. Wycliffe decided that he was not to be answered but after a moment Parkyn said, 'I've thought so for some time.'

'But done nothing about it.'

The major raised his huge shoulders in a slow shrug.

The man's detached omniscience was beginning to irritate. Wycliffe said, 'Well, it looks as though David has cleared out as you expected but Joe has been shot; did you expect that too?'

Parkyn did not bother to reply. He struck a match to re-light his pipe and held it poised. 'I think that Joe must have threatened him with the police. The last time I saw Joe he was a very worried man.'

'When was that?'

'Thursday evening, I think – yes, he was with me that evening and on Friday morning I looked in at the shop but he had a customer so I picked up his slip and left. I expected to see him again last night but he didn't turn up.'

The match burned down to his fingers; he threw it away and struck another. 'There was nothing unusual about that, our arrangements were always loose. However, when the shop didn't open this morning I began to wonder a bit and this evening I went along there. You know the rest.'

He put the match to his pipe at last and puffed it into life. Wycliffe wondered what the two men could have had in common. He had not met Joseph but from what he had heard and from the photograph in the sitting-room he had the impression of a timid, introspective individual, the sort who might be relied upon to follow in father's footsteps without protest, even with grati-tude. His whole existence had been bounded by the antique shop while Parkyn, despite Hetty's scorn, had played his part on a larger stage.

Another swig of whisky, another sigh. 'About my father's gun – is there any evidence that it was the gun which killed Joseph?'

'I'm waiting for a report from ballistics.'

It was odd. Wycliffe had an uncomfortable feeling that behind these exchanges it was he, Wycliffe, who was being shrewdly assessed and marked down. It annoyed him the more because he suspected that the feeling arose from his own absurd sense of inferiority. He told himself that by this time of night the man was seeing the world through an alcoholic haze. His movements were studied and slow and his eyes had acquired that glazed look which usually precedes sleep or the stupor that passes for sleep.

There was another loud creak from the passage and this time the door opened and Hetty stood there like a headmistress, ready to tear strips off an unruly class.

'Your supper is ready.'

Wycliffe stood up. 'I won't keep you.'

Parkyn saw him out and stood on the doorstep while he made his way down through the sodden garden to the road. It was still raining and the collar of his mackintosh felt clammily cold against his neck. He hurried down Dog's Leg Lane to the comparative cosiness of Bear Street. The old people knew how to build their streets so that they weren't wind tunnels. The fat woman's restaurant cast a pool of orange light over the road but the steamy windows made it impossible to see inside. He walked the length of the street to the harbour.

The lights of the police caravan were the only sign of habitation though navigation lights burned on the quay and at the mastheads of some of the moored craft. Reflections shimmered over the water.

The duty constable was reading a paperback.

'Anybody else in?'

'No, sir. Mr Scales is still with Dr Franks. Vanstone is keeping obo in Godolphin Street—'

A car drew up outside and Inspector Scales came in. 'I thought I might catch you.'

John Scales had been with Wycliffe for years, he was the backbone of the squad. He specialized in business and law but he was a first-class all-rounder as well.

'Anything from Franks?'

'Nothing helpful. He's fairly sure that Clement died on Saturday evening or during the night, he won't go further than that. The path of the bullet through the skull suggests that the gun was held with a considerable upward inclination – as it probably would have been if he shot himself.'

'Or if he was bending over his stamps when somebody shot him. I'd like to believe it was suicide, but the removal of the gun ... Did he say anything about the man's general health?'

'Good for a man of his age leading a rather too sedentary life. No sign of organic disease, no serious disabilities.'

They chatted for a few minutes and it was agreed that Scales should concentrate on the business side of the antique shop, through the accounts and by contacts with their bank manager and solicitor.

Wycliffe turned to the duty constable. 'I'm on my way home.'

But before going home he wanted another word with the woman in the restaurant and he walked down the street in the drizzling rain.

She was alone, clearing the tables. Gutted candles stood in a row on the counter with salt and pepper pots. He tried the door; it was locked but she saw him and let him in.

'You're all I need!'

'I won't keep you – just a couple of questions. Have you had a visit from my lads?'

She was grim. 'I have. One of them arrived while I was in the thick of it, following me round with his questions. I'm afraid I gave him short change. I know he's got his job to do but I've got my living to get . . . '

'I suppose you opened as usual on Saturday night?'

'It's our best night.'

'I wondered if you happened to notice anybody visiting opposite, say between seven-thirty and eight o'clock?'

She lowered her bulk on to one of the straw botto-med van Gogh chairs. 'If I don't take the weight off my feet I shall fall down.' She stooped to massage her ankles. 'Saturday evening . . . We had veal – veal cutlets done in white wine. We don't offer any choice of the main dish – one dish, but good, that's been our policy from the start. It was slack to begin with . . . ' She studied the rings on her soft, plump fingers. 'There *was* some-body, a bit before eight, I'd say. He came in a taxi and it was pouring with rain. After he'd paid off the taxi he couldn't get any answer at first, ringing at the side-door, then somebody came and let him in. I couldn't see who it was.'

A sound of whistling came from the kitchen and she grinned. 'My man, clearing up. He's only little but he's got go in him – more than I have. Anyway, about this chap, he was let in and that was the last I saw of him.'

'Can you tell me what he looked like?'

66

She frowned and pouted. 'I didn't see him all that well because he had his back to me most of the time but he was tall, and on the thin side.'

'Young?'

'Not exactly young – thirty-fivish, I'd say.'

'How was he dressed?'

'A dark mack – made of the stuff policemen wear, I think.'

'Hat?'

'No hat; he had dark hair – oh, and he was carrying a leather bag, like a large brief-case.'

'Were there any lights on in the shop?'

'No, I don't think so.'

'Did you see his face at all?'

'Well, I must have seen it but not clearly – he had a moustache.'

'And you didn't see this man leave?'

She shook her head. 'I didn't see him or anybody else after that except customers. We started to get busy and I didn't have time to look out of the window. Anyway, once this place fills up on a wet night you can't see because the windows get steamed over.'

'You've been a great help – thanks.'

'Is it true that they've both been murdered?'

'I told you, Joseph was found shot in his room upstairs.'

'And David?'

'I wish I knew. By the way, what's your name?'

'Blazek – Annie Blazek. I was a Drew before I married. My people are farmers over to Bere Alston.'

Taxis are a policeman's best friend. It was a simple matter to telephone headquarters and get them to put out a call for any driver who dropped a fare in Bear Street just before eight on Saturday evening. He used Annie's phone and that done he went back to his car and took the road for St Juliot and home.

If Joseph Clement had been shot on Saturday evening

then the visitor who, according to Molly Stokes, had come to sell something, was very much in the picture along with brother David.

Toby Williams, the boatman, lived in one of the row of cottages whose long, narrow gardens reached down to the shore. It was almost eleven but there was a light in his downstair room and Wycliffe picked his way down three or four steps to the front door. When he knocked it was opened almost at once by Toby himself.

Toby was a little barrel of a man. As always he wore a sailor's blue jersey but Wycliffe now saw him for the first time without his cap which had left a red line just below the line of his sparse grey hair. He had a splendidly lush moustache and a small tuft of hair on his chin.

'The wife's gone to bed; she can't keep 'er eyes open after ten and that's just when I begins to wake up.'

'Give the man a drink, Toby!' A West African grey parrot in his cage watched Wycliffe with a beady eye, standing first on one leg then on the other.

Toby laughed. 'Beer, Mr Wycliffe?' There were two glasses on the table ready with a quart jug of beer. 'I brews me own an' I can say 'tis better than the cat's piss they sell in pubs.'

The parlour was small and Wycliffe's head scarcely cleared the ceiling beams but it was cosy. A fire burned in the tiny grate.

'I want to get in touch with David Clement so if he's gone off in the *Manna*, we need to find her.'

Toby took a gulp of beer. 'Your health, Mr Wycliffe.'

'Bottoms up!' The parrot said.

'Clement left a note?'

Toby reached for a crumpled sheet of paper which had been wedged between two ornaments on the mantelpiece. 'This is it; I searched through the rubbish after you rung.'

It was a sheet of paper with the firm's printed heading

and a scribbled note written with a ball-point. 'I've taken *Manna* from her moorings – D.C.'

'I suppose it *is* his writing?'

Toby scratched his head. 'God knows, Mr Wycliffe! You can't expect me to know how they all write.'

'Has he taken the boat out before at night?'

'Not as I remember. Some of 'em do though.'

'What sort of trip would she be capable of? Could she cross the channel, for instance?'

'Oh, yes. No problem. You could take 'er almost anywhere in reason. She's a good sea boat and Clement knows 'ow to 'andle 'er. I'll say that for 'n.'

'What about fuel?'

'Well, 'e wouldn't cross the channel with what she was carrying, that's for sure. Without filling up 'e might make forty mile – no more.'

'She was moored off; how did he get out to her?'

'The dinghy was kept upturned on the shingle at the bottom of my garden an' rowlocks and oars was in my shed. Each one of my owners 'as got 'is own sort of rack in the shed.'

'Can you give me a description of *Manna*?'

Toby got up from his chair and went to the sideboard where he rummaged in one of the drawers and came up with a snapshot. 'That's *Manna*, Mr Wycliffe, my gran'son took that.'

It showed the boat clearly enough with Toby's bulk poised in the act of climbing over the side into the dinghy.

'The young devil said 'e thought I was going to fall in an' 'e wanted something to remember me by.' He added, 'You can see 'er lines an' I can tell 'e anything else you want to know.'

Wycliffe took down a detailed description of *Manna* and by that time the banjo-clock on the wall was showing ten minutes to twelve. Toby saw him to the door and the parrot said, 'Don't 'e bother to come back.'

Toby apologized. ''Tis only a bird, Mr Wycliffe, 'e don't understand.'

Helen was in their living-room, reading. 'Have you had a meal this evening?'

'No, but I had a good lunch. You go to bed, you shouldn't have waited up.'

'There's some cold chicken.'

'A little chicken with a slice of bread and a cup of tea would do me very well.'

The man in the taxi was certainly the man who had come to sell the Clement brothers something and the marked catalogue, open on the desk, suggested that the something might be glass paperweights. High quality bijouterie; small, easily portable and reasonably negotiable; a man could carry a fortune in his briefcase.

But what had gone wrong? Whatever it was, Joseph was dead and his brother had cleared off in *Manna*. That left the visitor and David's car unaccounted for. It was tempting to link the two. Was it credible that the visitor had dropped David off at the quay then driven away in David's car? It covered the broad facts.

Glass paperweights.

He remembered having seen something about them recently but could not recall the context.

Baccarat, Millefiori, Clichy, St Louis ... Beautiful things, beautiful names ... The sounds had a soothing, soporific effect ...

'Charles!'

For a moment he had no idea where he was then he saw Helen bending over him. He was lolling on the settee and there was a trolley at his elbow with supper.

'You dropped off; you must be exhausted.'

CHAPTER FOUR

Tuesday morning was fine with blue skies and fleecy white clouds but there was a nip in the air, a reminder that spring had not yet truly arrived. Even so police headquarters was unusually cheerful, everybody greeted everybody else with a complacent grin as though claiming some part in the improvement.

The local paper was on his desk. 'City Antique Dealer found Shot – Murder say Police.' The police had said no such thing but some oracle in the chief's office had announced in the usual bland gobbledygook: 'The possibility of foul play cannot be excluded at this stage.' But Clement's disappearance and the absence of *Manna* from her moorings would keep the press busy for a while; they might even help to find them both.

Among reports was one from Melville of Ballistics. Melville had done a thorough job at the cost of a night's sleep. There were photographs taken with a comparison microscope showing, side by side, different views of the bullet recovered from Joseph's room and one newly fired from the gun Wycliffe had found on the beach. In Melville's opinion both had been fired from the same gun; in other words, Joseph had been killed with the general's gun.

A bit of firm ground.

And it seemed that the watch on Molly Stokes might be about to pay off. Molly had returned to the flats at seven that morning off night-duty and at eight a taxi had arrived. A minute or two later Molly came out, smartly dressed, and carrying a week-end case. Crowther was keeping observation from a parked van and he followed her taxi to the railway station where she took a ticket to Bournemouth.

The duty C.I.D. officer immediately asked Bournemouth police to tail her on arrival and a description given over the telephone was followed by a picture by wire.

Of course it was possible that the girl was going to spend a day or two with friends but it seemed unlikely that she would leave home at this time unless her trip were in some way connected with Clement's disappearance. If Clement was operating on the wrong side of the law it was possible that they had arranged a rendezvous – not specifically for this occasion but in case things went badly wrong at any time.

Wycliffe telephoned the Horton Radford. 'Is it possible to speak to Nurse Molly Stokes?'

A plummy voice, accustomed to soothing the jangled nerves of top people, said, 'Staff-nurse Stokes went off duty at six-thirty this morning and she is not due back until mid-day on Thursday.'

So she had not thrown up her job and it looked as though she would be back in a couple of days; by which time he hoped to be in a position to call any bluff she chose to try.

He spent a few minutes editing Toby's description of *Manna*, then handed it over for circulation to port authorities and coast-guards on both sides of the Channel. That done, he called Sergeant Bourne, his administrative officer, on the internal telephone.

'These so-called "art-robberies" in the stockbroker belt round London – I suppose you've got copies of the missing-property lists put out by the Met?'

'Yes, sir. They've been circulated to all dealers in our area.'

'Bring the copies to my office, please.'

Bourne was an extremely efficient young man; his soul yearned for administrative perfection. No doubt he

72

prayed daily in the computer room: 'Thy Kingdom come; Thy Will be done.' No doubt either he would one day rise to the top of the hierarchy where such qualities were increasingly valued. But Wycliffe could not learn to love him any more than he loved foam-plastic bread or reconstituted, hydrated ham. Wycliffe was not in harmony with his time, neither was he enamoured of those who were.

Bourne came in, correct and assured, a fine pinstripe; hairstyle, a perfect compromise between short-back-and-sides and the trendy; two copies of the lists in his hand.

'Sit down, Bourne.'

Wycliffe leafed through one of the lists. 'In total it makes a tidy haul, doesn't it?'

'Fourteen break-ins over the past two years with a total insurance loss of more than three hundred and eighty thousand pounds.'

'Thank God it isn't on our patch! All small stuff?'

'Small but valuable. Snuff boxes, vinaigrettes, miniatures, medallions . . . '

'Glass paperweights?'

'The very last list, sir. A collection of glass paperweights valued at nearly twenty thousand pounds, most of them purchased by the owner at a London auction only a few months earlier.'

Wycliffe turned the pages to the appropriate list. Twenty-six weights in all. He usually looked through the missing property lists when they arrived from another force and a glance now left him in no doubt that this was where he had first seen the evocative descriptions: 'A Baccarat patterned concentric millefiori primrose weight . . . A St Louis faceted mushroom weight . . . A St Louis concentric millefiori shamrock weight . . .' He picked up the internal telephone and dialled.

'D.C. Trice?'

D.C. Trice was a blonde enlisted under the sex-equality

banner with some misgiving but she was good at her job.

' . . . The stuff brought back from the antique shop . . . The sale catalogue that was open on the desk – will you read out the marked items on the page at which it was open? . . . Slowly! I want to check them against a list . . .'

Bourne listened to Wycliffe's side of the conversation with interest. When it was over Bourne said, 'The Clement brothers were fencing the stuff, is that it?'

'All six items marked in the catalogue were on the Met's stolen property list. It seems that the Saturday night visitor had come to fence part of the haul and in order to come to terms they were checking against the sale prices.'

Bourne was delighted. 'In that case he must have been in on the robberies and that will be news for the Met.'

News which Bourne would be anxious to pass on himself, laying up treasure in heaven.

'If we get a reasonable description from the taxi driver you can put it on the telex then get hold of whoever is in charge of the case at the Met and put him wise personally.'

Bourne was eager. 'We've already got the taxi driver's statement, he was in an hour ago. I brought a copy with me.' He handed over a typewritten slip.

The description tallied with what Annie Blazek had told him as far as that went. Tall, slight of build, dark with moustache and sideburns. Aged about thirty-five. He carried a brown leather case and the driver had picked him up at West Hill station among the passengers off the London train at 19.25 and taken him direct to the antique shop.

'Well, that's it, Bourne. Good hunting!'

Bourne paused for a moment at the door with a backward glance. He was never quite sure when the mickey was being taken.

The case was on the move. Either the motor cruiser

had taken fuel aboard or she had not gone far. They were now looking for the motor cruiser, a car and two men – David Clement and his visitor. The more the merrier; time to worry when there were no leads.

Wycliffe glanced through the reports of house-to-house enquiries in Bear Street which were still in progress. So far they were not encouraging; the shops on either side of the antique shop were lock-ups with no-one living over and this applied to most of the premises in the street which was essentially a business area. Joseph had probably shot himself or been shot at some time between eight o'clock when Annie saw the visitor being admitted and, say, one in the morning. The gun had been dropped on the beach at St Juliot at some time after two and the fishermen had seen a car backing off the quay at about half-past.

He settled to a morning's desk work and was interrupted by John Scales.

'I've talked to the bank manager. A bit sticky at first but he came round. The affairs of Clement Brothers Antiques don't look too rosy. Turnover and profits have been falling and Perrins – the bank manager – thinks that in a year or so they would have been finished. He blames David. Under the elder brother the business made steady though not handsome profits. Incidentally, there is no sign of all the business David is supposed to have done on his travels. Cash transactions I imagine – no records, no tax, no questions.

'Anyway, I asked about a solicitor and the bank manager referred me to Lambert Parkes and Davis. He remembered that they had acted for Joseph's father. I saw Mr Davis, a smug individual who was reluctant to say more than "Good morning!" When I pointed out that we were probably dealing with a murder case he condescended to tell me that they had received no instructions from Joseph since the proving of his father's will. Presumably there was a deed of partnership when he took David into the business but if there was Mr Davis did not draw it up.'

They chatted for a while then Scales said, 'It looks as though Clement and his visitor drove to St Juliot early Sunday morning. Clement went aboard his boat leaving the other chap with the car. When the fishermen saw the car backing off the quay, Clement must have been on his boat, waiting for the coast to clear before putting to sea.'

Wycliffe sighed. 'I suppose that makes sense but still there's the problem of the gun.' He shifted irritably in his chair. 'I don't think we've got it right, John – not yet.'

The scene-of-crime reports arrived – a file in themselves. They included a scale plan of the dead man's room, a score of photographs, an inventory and a detailed account of the examination that had been made. Most of this was for the courts if it ever got that far but the section on fingerprints interested him.

The telephone and the door handles of the office doors carried no prints – they had been wiped clean. The door to the yard carried one set. Some joker (surely not Smith?) had made the most of these; 'they were those of a known person, viz: Chief Detective Superintendent Wycliffe.' Two sets of prints had turned up in profusion all over the building, the dead man's and, presumably, his brother's.

Wycliffe could think of no reason why David Clement should have wiped his prints off the telephone and the door knobs so, presumably, the wiping had been done for, and perhaps by, somebody else. The Saturday night visitor? It was an attractive idea.

On the brass handle of the old safe there were blurred prints – quite unidentifiable. In another part of the report the contents of the safe were listed and these came as a surprise. They included two gold snuff boxes and a couple of ivory figurines – not on any lists of stolen property, as well as fifteen hundred pounds in cash. If

Clement cleared out voluntarily was it likely that he would have left all that behind? The answer seemed to be an emphatic No! But the inference – where did that lead?

Wycliffe had lunch in the Bear Street restaurant for no better reason than a need to establish a routine appropriate to the case. This was his way; every new case found him trying to fit his actions as far as possible into a routine. Only then did he feel free to devote his whole energy to the problems on hand. He could not have explained it any more than he could explain why he always walked on the cracks in the pavement or invariably put on the right before the left leg of his trousers when dressing. Yet he had never hated his father or despised his mother.

He was early and the fat woman had not started to serve.

'What is it today?'

'Beef casserole with boiled potatoes and carrots.'

'Good!' But not for weight watching.

'I'll bring you your lager.'

Afterwards he looked in at the incident van by the harbour and glanced through three or four reports which had just come in. D.C. Dixon was duty officer.

'Anything in these?'

'Two things, sir. A woman who lives over the shop next but one to the antique shop says she was awakened on Saturday night by a car being started and driven down the back lane. She sleeps in the back of the house, sir.'

'Has she any idea of the time?'

'All she can say is that it was after one because she'd been reading in bed and she didn't put the light out until a few minutes to one. She thinks she went to sleep almost at once and that she was awakened not long afterwards.'

'And the other report?'

'From the landlord of the *Seven Stars*, sir. He says that David Clement came into his bar just before nine on Saturday evening. He bought a packet of cigarettes, had a beer, and stayed about twenty minutes.'

'Is he a regular there?'

'No. The landlord says he comes in occasionally when he's run out of cigarettes after the shops have shut; then he has a drink to make it look right.'

'Is he sure of the time?'

'Apparently. They have a TV in the bar and Clement came in while they were waiting for *Dallas* to start.' Dixon, uncertain of his chief's acquaintance with the classics of TV, added, 'It's a show about Texas, sir.'

So far this was the last occasion on which anyone had admitted having seen Clement.

He drove back to headquarters through the chaotic traffic of the city centre and arrived at his office just in time to take a call from Kersey. Kersey had gone to St Juliot in response to a report that David's car had been found at the bottom of the disused quarry, about three hundred yards off the road through the village.

'Driven over the edge deliberately, sir – a drop of forty feet . . . Yes, I've been down, there's nobody in it . . . Smith is with me . . . No, it won't be too difficult to get it up, I've sent for the recovery truck . . . '

So much for the idea that Clement had gone off in his boat and the visitor in his car.

Wycliffe said, 'So it's possible that the two of them went off in the cruiser.'

Kersey seemed doubtful. 'I suppose so, but why go to the trouble of ditching the car?'

'It was hidden. Left on the quay or in the village it would soon have raised questions. As it is, if it wasn't for the gun on the beach we might still not be in on the act. Somebody was buying time.'

It occurred to Wycliffe as he dropped the phone that Clement might, after all, have gone to St Juliot alone, driven the car on to the quay, unloaded his baggage, ditched the car and then boarded his boat.

Leaving a small fortune, easily portable, in the safe? It hardly seemed likely. Perhaps he panicked? But he was calm enough to write a note which made sure that Toby Williams would not raise the alarm when he saw that *Manna* was missing from her moorings.

Wycliffe turned to the little pile of documents on his desk awaiting signature but almost immediately he was interrupted by Sergeant Bourne.

'I passed on the news to the Met, sir. The officer in charge of the case is Chief Inspector Worth and he's quite chuffed. It's the first promising lead they've had and he's sending down a Sergeant Minns by train with a special mug book – cons not at present in gaol but with the right kind of form for these jobs. Minns is due in at three.'

'You'd better get hold of the taxi driver and Annie Blazek. Bring them here with Minns when he arrives.'

Bourne went off, tail high.

Wycliffe thought, 'Too much happening – the storm before the lull.' If the case ran true to form they would be biting their nails for days after this.

Bourne collected Sergeant Minns from the station and picked up the taxi driver and Annie on his way.

The taxi driver had first go with the mug book, seated at the table in Bourne's office, watched by Bourne and the Met sergeant. After a while they were joined by Wycliffe. It was routine, but routine which often carried with it a measure of suspense. The driver, a plump, comfortable man, reading glasses half-way down his nose, took his time, turning the pages slowly, studying the photographs with care and occasionally going back for a second look. Finally, about two-thirds of the way through the book he stopped and said, 'I think that's the man.'

Bourne told him there was no hurry, that he could go

through the whole book again, but the man was firm in his choice. 'No, that's him all right. I know it was raining and dark but I saw him plain enough in the lights under the station canopy.'

Minns was delighted and when the taxi driver had left the room with Bourne to sign a formal statement he said, 'George Alfred Waddington, sir. Two-year suspended sentence for burglary in '68 and a five year stretch in '71 – both country-house jobs badly bungled. Now Alfie seems to have lined up with a brainier mob. He's a wizard with alarm systems and that's the only reason why they would use him. Outside of that he must be a pain in the neck.'

Annie came in and took her place at the table with the mug book. She cast a shy, rather nervous glance at Wycliffe, intimidated by her surroundings. But she soon settled down and spent a long time turning the pages of the album with her plump, ringed fingers. In the end she couldn't make up her mind between two men. 'I think it's one of them, Mr Wycliffe, but I can't honestly be sure.'

Waddington was one of the two she had chosen and that was enough for Minns.

'I'd better get back as soon as possible, sir. We shouldn't have any trouble picking him up. We know his haunts and he can't know we're after him.'

Wycliffe was by no means so confident but he said nothing.

Annie had continued to turn the pages of the mug book and suddenly she said, 'That's David Clement!'

It was not a mug-shot but one of a number of shots in the back of the album, apparently taken in bars. It showed four men seated round a table in front of them.

Minns turned to Wycliffe, 'What on earth is she talking about?'

Wycliffe explained and Minns went on, 'Those shots were taken by our undercover boys of meetings between known criminals with the right M.O. for these art jobs. Just in case something might click.' He grinned. 'Naturally, we don't ask their permission or let them catch us at it if we can help it. Even the landlords of the pubs aren't too keen if they find out what we're up to.'

Annie was looking at Wycliffe with eyes that were almost pleading. 'I really ought to get back . . . '

'Yes, of course.' He took her to Bourne and arranged for her to make her statement. 'Mr Bourne will see that you are taken home and thank you for your help.'

Back in the office he asked Minns if the three men with Clement were known.

'I'll say! That's the point. One is Waddington and the other two have form for housebreaking; their mug-shots are in the album too. The man you say is Clement isn't known to us but if he's not a villain himself then he's picked some dandy playmates.' Minns could scarcely conceal his satisfaction. 'With a bit of luck this should wrap the whole thing up.'

'We shall want first call on this man Waddington.'

Minns nodded but without conviction. 'Waddington is no killer, Mr Wycliffe, you can take that from me; all the same, I'll mention it to my guv'nor.'

'So will I, Sergeant. So will I.' Wycliffe was looking at the photograph which included David Clement. 'When and where was this taken?'

Minns turned to an index sheet. 'It was taken last January in the lounge bar of a pub in St John's Wood; quite a respectable place. These chaps fancy themselves; they reckon they've got class; no third-rate boozers for them. Waddington, for instance, has taught himself to speak proper and he plays golf at the weekends.'

Wycliffe smiled. 'It looks as though we've got interests in common, Sergeant.'

Minns closed his album. 'You can say that again, sir. So if that's all, I'll be getting back. If I put my skates on I could make the 17.52. The sooner we get moving the better.'

81

'I agree. Mr Bourne will arrange for you to be taken to the station. Thank you for your help and my compliments to Chief Inspector Worth.'

Inter-force co-operation; everybody agrees that it is a splendid thing – absolutely essential. And everybody goes about it tongue-in-cheek or at least with fingers crossed, especially when it involves the Met.

Alone, he went back to his office with the photographs Minns had left so that copies could be made – the shot of Clement with his cronies in the pub and the mug-shot of Waddington.

David Clement had joined his brother in the business about three years since. Before that he had worked in a London insurance office, now he was consorting with known criminals and handling nice little portable antiques which, if not worth their weight in gold were moving in that direction. It could be made to hang together.

From what he had heard of Waddington he was even less inclined to believe that Clement had cleared out in his company and he had not even suggested the possibility to Minns.

Five o'clock. Diane came in with a neat folder of letters to be signed.

Sometimes he envied people with jobs where they knew exactly what they had to do. Their days had a beginning, a middle and an end. One might take a pride in doing such a job well. He seemed to spend his time floundering in a welter of activity which might come to something or nothing. Only rarely was it possible to go home at the end of the day with any feeling of completion, there was always the carry-over to tomorrow. But when he confided such thoughts to Helen he got little sympathy. 'It's what you live for. Goodness knows what will happen when you eventually retire.'

The telephone rang and Diane answered it. She put

her hand over the mouthpiece. 'Superintendent Redfern from Bournemouth on the line.'

'Tell them to put him through.' He took the receiver. 'Hullo, Jimmy! Any news for me?' They were old friends, having survived several courses and conferences together.

'About your girl, Charles. She arrived on schedule and our chap tailed her. She walked to Canning Terrace in the area behind Central Station where there are three or four blocks of flats. She went to one of these – Gort House – and took the lift to the fourth floor. My chap took a chance and went up with her, pretending to be calling on someone on the same floor. She had a key to Flat C on that floor and she went in. After about fifteen minutes she was out again but without her weekend case. She then took a leisurely stroll to the town centre and had a late lunch in a restaurant. Since then she's done a bit of window shopping and bought some food in a supermarket.'

Wycliffe's thanks were sincere. Having done his share of foot-slogging surveillance he knew the amount of patience and skill needed to gain that amount of information without being spotted.

'Do you want to keep it up, Charles?'

'I'd be grateful.'

'No problem. We're fairly quiet at the moment, holding our breath until the season starts. Incidentally, I made a few inquiries about Flat C on the fourth. It's leased to one Alan Page, said to be some sort of salesman or commercial rep. It's small, just a bedroom, living-room, kitchen and usual offices.'

'Thanks again.'

He finished with the paperwork to Diane's satisfaction and she whisked it away. An empty desk.

He was pleased with what Redfern had told him. The flat in Bournemouth was just the bolt-hole he had hoped to find. All that was needed now was for Clement to turn up there.

And what if he did?

Did he really believe that David Clement had murdered his brother? If not – if Joseph had committed suicide, what was all the fuss about? The art robberies were not his business. He had found a loaded gun on the beach and from that a case had mushroomed, but what was the case?

He stood at the window of his office which overlooked one of the main highways out of the city. The evening exodus was beginning. Suddenly he felt depressed.

There was a tap at the door and it opened. 'Oh, there you are, Charles!' Hugh Annesley Bellings, the deputy chief constable. As though it was a surprise to find him in his own office. Bellings was tall, lean, handsome and suave. He was, as Wycliffe thought of him, 'the other kind of copper' – really an administrator like Bourne, but Bourne with Winchester and Balliol behind him. He sat in his office reading and annotating reports, studying statistics and musing on trends. His greatest concern was the public image of the force.

'I've read your reports, Charles. Odd case, isn't it?'

Bellings never discussed a case as such, only in terms of its possible political, social or personal implications. Wycliffe wondered which it would be this time.

'I met the elder Clement once – rather an uncouth sort of chap I thought, but he knew about furniture. I was offered a little Carlton House table at what seemed a reasonable price but a friend advised me to let Clement have a look at it before buying. Luckily I did. The thing had been cannibalised and he picked it up at once.' Bellings smiled in gracious acknowledgement of his own fallibility. 'Of course, that was years ago, before this brother came into the business.'

Wycliffe contented himself with looking bland and saying nothing.

'I've noticed that Gavin Parkyn's name keeps crop-
ping up in the reports.'

They had arrived; this was the reason for the visit.

'You know him?'

A foolish question. Just as Wycliffe and his colleagues
studied to know every villain on their patch, so Bellings
made a similar effort to acquaint himself with everyone
of rank, wealth or of any kind of distinction, from the
patrician vice-chancellor of the university, to the
scaffolding-to-boardroom chairman of Purvis Construc-
tions; from the Lord Mayor of the city to the little chit of
a girl who was spoken of as a possible for the athletics
team in the next Olympics.

Bellings drew in his lips. 'I can't say that I *know* him; I
doubt if anyone does and in any case I have had very
little contact with him since we were young men serving
together in Korea.'

It was the first time Wycliffe had heard of the deputy's
active service experience. 'In the marines?'

'A marine commando unit, yes. We were together for
just a few months and since then I have only met him a
couple of times though, of course, I have heard quite a
lot about him.' Bellings studied his long thin hands in
reflective mood. 'He was a strange character. We called
him Moggy Parkyn because he seemed to have at least as
many lives as a cat. He was totally regardless of his own
safety – but totally! One supposed that he either
believed in a charmed existence or cared nothing for his
life. But it was after the Korean affair, when he resigned
his commission, that his career really began. He transferred to Intelligence and worked in Europe. The work he
did in that field in the late fifties and through the sixties
and seventies is still very little talked about but he was, I
understand, a key figure in Western counter-espionage.'

'You surprise me.'

Bellings laughed and was gratified. 'I can see that. My
dear fellow! You musn't be misled by what he seems to

be now. Do you know that he speaks five langauges with impeccable fluency – including Russian?'

Wycliffe said nothing and Bellings went on, 'I'm glad I came to see you, Charles – glad that I was able to put you in the picture. Now that you know . . . '

It was part of the Bellings technique to leave sentences in the air so that he did not have to make points with vulgar directness or commit himself further than was necessary.

Wycliffe straightened the objects on his desk, a sure sign to those who knew him that he was about to be obstinate. 'I have no reason to think that Parkyn is criminally involved in this business but his association with the Clement brothers means that he must be questioned like anybody else and, after all, Joseph was shot with the general's gun.'

'Stolen by the younger brother.'

'Possibly, but Parkyn himself acknowledges that he was a regular caller at the shop; he went there each morning to collect Joseph's betting slip, and the two met in the evenings at least twice a week.' He paused, then went on, 'Whatever Parkyn may have been in the past his present interests seem to be gambling on horses and stupefying himself with alcohol.' Even as he spoke Wycliffe experienced a twinge of conscience in thus describing the major.

Bellings shifted in his chair and Wycliffe knew that he was needled. 'I've heard something of the sort; he seems to have taken to an eccentric way of life, but I expect the sudden break – the abrupt transition from stress and even danger, to the humdrum existence of a man on pension – has been difficult to cope with. However, what I am saying, Charles, is that despite his idiosyncracies it is unthinkable that a man like Parkyn could be involved in a sordid little crime. And what is more, anything that looked in the least like harassment on our part could have serious repercussions at the highest level. However he lives, Parkyn still has sufficient influence—'

'To be immune from the ordinary processes of police investigation?'

For once Bellings lost his cool. 'Don't be ridiculous, Charles! You seem to have a grudge against the man!'

The interview ended as most exchanges between the two men did with irritation on both sides. Bellings was annoyed because he had been forced to spell out his message to no apparent purpose; Wycliffe was annoyed for more complex reasons which included the fact that Bellings always manoeuvred him into betraying a strain of priggishness in his nature.

Bellings stood up. 'Well, it's your case, Charles.'

'Yes, it is.'

Wycliffe could imagine him muttering under his breath, 'Uncouth fellow!'

But he was more troubled by the remark he had actually heard: 'You seem to have a grudge against the man!' It annoyed him that he had so far shown his feelings that Bellings was able to read something special in his attitude to Parkyn. Of course it was absurd to suggest that he bore the major any grudge; the truth was more subtle and more complex. His attitude owed something to recollections of childhood, something to his sense of inferiority which put him on the defensive but much more to the fact that Parkyn's way of life seemed to express that particular brand of disillusionment which sometimes threatened his own peace of mind. 'There, but for the grace of God . . . ' And he was by no means sure of that. 'I'm feeling my age,' he told himself.

He had planned an early night, an evening by the fire with Helen; a book or the television. But he knew that if he went home now he would spend the evening moping, a menace to Helen's peace of mind as well as his own. He reached for the telephone and asked for his home number.

'Is that you? . . . I'm afraid I shall be late . . . I've got nothing done today and there's a stack of stuff . . . No, don't save food for me, I'll get something . . . '

It was true; there was always a stack of paperwork waiting to be done but if Bellings . . .

He took a bulky file from a drawer of his desk: *Proposals for a new Command Structure with Observations on Staffing.*

The headquarters building was emptying and the familiar background noises gave way to an unnatural stillness. Odd that police headquarters should maintain only a skeleton staff during the hours when sixty percent of crimes are committed. Outside the flow of traffic dropped to a trickle and soon only single cars disturbed the silence. At a little after seven he switched on his desk lamp. He had waded through about a fifth of the file and annotated a good deal of it. A pall of grey smoke hung over his desk, rising slowly until it was caught and whisked away by the erratic air-conditioning. He was beginning to feel at peace with himself once more, fit to mix with other human beings. He had told Helen not to keep a meal so he telephoned the restaurant in Bear Street and spoke to Annie.

'I expect we can manage one extra; what time are you coming?'

'Say, eight o'clock.'

At a quarter to eight he stopped work, cleared his desk and fetched his coat from the cloakroom. He was leaving his office when the telephone rang.

'A woman from the restaurant in Bear Street, sir. She says she was speaking to you earlier—'

'Put her through.'

'Oh, it's you at last!' Annie was almost inarticulate with excitement. 'He's here again – outside the antique shop. The man who came on Saturday evening – he's ringing the bell at the side-door . . . '

'Can you see him now?'

'Yes, he's—'

'Don't ring off.' He got Information Room on the inter-com and gave instructions for cars in the neighbourhood of Bear Street to intercept. 'Detain for questioning suspect at present outside Clement's antique shop in Bear Street. Description . . . ' He recited the description which was now firmly fixed in his mind. 'Stop me if I go wrong, Annie . . . Have you go that? . . . All right, get on with it but keep this line open. Can you still see him, Annie? . . . Good! They shouldn't be long . . . '

He looked at the wall clock; the seconds hand seemed to race round the dial. Annie reported that her man had moved from the side-door to the door of the shop and was tapping on the glass. How long would he keep trying?

'What?'

Annie told him that a police car had arrived. Another interval. 'What did you say? . . . Good! Any trouble? . . . That's fine, and thank you. You've saved us a great deal of bother.'

He spoke to Information Room again. 'Tell them to take the suspect to Mallet Street.' Mallet Street police station was only an estate agent's stone-throw from the antique shop.

Five minutes to eight. Sergeant Minns would still be in the train on his way back to London. Childish to laugh. He picked up his car and drove to Mallet Street. Kersey was already there.

'I heard the kerfuffle on the car radio.'

Every living creature has an environment to which it is best suited, in which it looks and feels most at home; from the koala bear in its gum tree to the virtuoso conductor on his rostrum. For George Alfred Wadding-ton that optimum was a bar stool with a double whisky in front of him and a busty barmaid to chat up. In the aseptic bleakness of a police interview room he was lost.

'Mr Waddington? George Alfred Waddington?'

'Yes, but I should like to know—'

Seen in a good light Waddington was a poor specimen; round shouldered, skin and bone. Not so long ago he would have been written off as 'consumptive.' Yet he was a dandy with his trendy moustache, his sideburns and his well-cut grey pinstripe.

'Where have you been since Saturday evening?'

The pale brown eyes were evasive. 'Since Saturday?'

'Isn't that when you arrived here? On the train from town which got in at seven twenty-five in the evening – isn't that right?'

'Well—'

Whatever his skill with security devices Waddington wasn't bright.

'Simple, straightforward question – where have you been since then?'

'At my hotel, the *Unicorn* in Duke Street.'

'Evidently you haven't been keeping up with the local news, Mr Waddington.'

'I don't know what you're talking about.'

Wycliffe was more than half convinced that he didn't. There had been nothing about the case on the radio or television and nothing in the national press.

'Joseph Clement has been shot and his brother has disappeared.'

Waddington was shaken but he mustered all his intelligence and put on a bold front, 'Who are they?'

'Strange!' Wycliffe made a strategic pause to fill his pipe, a leisurely business, watched by the poor devil as though it were some sort of sacrament. 'You went straight from the railway station to their shop on Saturday night and you were ringing their door-bell again this evening but you don't know who they are.'

'I've nothing to say.' He'd made it at last but far too late.

It was Kersey's turn. 'A bit of business involving glass paper-weights. You see! We don't need you to talk, we *know*. You've got form, Waddington, two convictions, and it looks as though you were the last person to see Joseph Clement alive.'

'Christ! You're not saying I killed him?'

'Didn't you? Anyway, let's get back to what you were doing at the shop on Saturday evening.'

Wycliffe said, 'Mr Waddington won't mind if we take a look in his bag.'

Kersey picked up the bag and snapped it open then he began lifting out the contents on to the table. 'Pyjamas, sponge-bag, electric razor, tissues . . . brush and comb . . . What's this, then?'

A pair of socks turned inside out over some hard and heavy object which, unwrapped, proved to be a glass paperweight in its chamois-leather pouch. And there were three more in Waddington's laundry.

Kersey said, 'It beats me how you've managed to stay out of gaol so long.'

Waddington looked at the four weights, gleaming in the light, and said nothing.

'And there's still the shooting.'

'But I swear—'

'I shouldn't bother to swear, just tell us what happened when you went to the antique shop on Saturday evening.'

Waddington looked bleakly round the bare little room, knowing that he was destined to see a good many more like it in the future.

Time for the famous caution, part of the British legal handicapping system. 'You are not obliged to say anything but anything you do say may be taken down and given in evidence.'

Waddington sighed. 'What's the use? The long and short of it is, Clement wanted out and the others didn't see it that way. If he went, we were washed up.'

'Because he was the brains.'

'Not altogether. He had inside information on these

91

houses and he was in the trade with the right connections for fencing the stuff but that was all.'

'Clement set up the jobs and fenced the proceeds – but that was all. What more did you want? Anyway, what *I* want is to know exactly what happened at the antique shop on Saturday evening.'

Waddington had given up. 'Well, Clement had set up the paperweight job before backing out so we had the stuff on our hands.'

'Go on.'

'Well, the others – my associates – fixed for me to bring the weights down here and ask him to find a buyer.'

'And if he refused?'

Waddington hesitated. 'I was to hint that he might find himself in trouble with you lot.'

Kersey said, 'I can see why they picked on you. So, there you were, standing out in the rain with fifteen thousand quid's worth of glass burning a hole in your little bag. What happened?'

'I didn't know the chap who let me in but he said he was Clement's brother. He took me to an office at the back and asked me a lot of questions but I wasn't sure where he stood in the business so I played dumb. Then Dave turned up and the brother pushed off without another word.'

'What was David Clement's attitude when you'd said your little piece?'

'Oh, he didn't seem bothered. He said he thought he might have a customer but that it would take a day or two and that I was to come back on Tuesday – that's tonight.'

'I asked him what he thought I was going to do meanwhile and he said he'd fix me up in a quiet pub where I could lie low and keep out of the way.'

Waddington ran a hand through his dark hair. 'In the end I had to go along with that but it was when he said,

"You'll have to leave the weights, nobody's going to buy that sort of thing blind," I said that wasn't on and he just waved his hands and said, "Piss off then and catch your train."

'I didn't know what to do so I rang . . . I rang one of my associates and he spoke to Clement. After a bit of arguing they agreed that I should leave two of the weights and hold on to four.'

Wycliffe said, 'Did you see anybody while you were in the shop except the two brothers?'

'Nobody.'

'What time did you leave?'

'Coming up for a quarter to nine. David fixed me up at the *Unicorn* by phone.'

'Why did you wipe your dabs off the telephone and the door knobs?'

He looked blank. 'I don't know what you're on about; I never wiped off any dabs. I didn't know somebody was going to get done there, did I?'

So much for the Saturday night visitor. What Waddington had said turned a certain amount of speculation into fact and some of his statements could be checked. At least, David Clement's role was now clear. With knowledge gained from his work in insurance he had set up a number of robberies and used the cover of the antique business to sell stolen goods. But there are limits to the value of such inside information, however valuable in the first place. Clement had banked on a short but profitable career in crime and it seemed that the time had come for him to retire. But had he done so on his own terms?

CHAPTER FIVE

April is a fickle month and on Wednesday morning a southerly gale blew up the estuary bringing frequent rain squalls with intervals when the sun shone down on a turbulent sea flecked with white foam.

'Take your heavy mackintosh, not your raincoat.'

'I'm not going trekking across country.'

'No, but take it all the same.'

He was tired and not in the best of tempers. The headquarters building looked blatantly bleak. The glass and concrete pile, brain-child of a distinguished architect of the sixties, triumphed over the landscape in mindless assertiveness. He spurned the lift and ran up the stairs three at a time, an example of what the psychologists call displacement activity.

Before taking off his coat he called Bourne on the internal phone.

'Bourne? . . . Yes, that's what I'm ringing about. Any word from the Met? . . . Oh, Minns again; you'd better tell him to get a season ticket . . . No, I leave him to you . . . I don't care a damn about Waddington except in so far as our case is concerned . . . '

The truth was that he felt disappointed and frustrated. When Annie Blazek had telephoned to say that the Saturday night caller was back it had seemed for a moment that all might be over bar the paperwork but half-an-hour with Waddington had brought disillusionment. Everything pointed to Waddington being a small-time crook who had been taken up by a few of the bigger boys because of his skill with alarm systems. It had been Waddington's bad luck to get caught up in the drama of the Clement brothers which, almost certainly, had nothing to do with him.

The drama of the Clement brothers; here he was back to the beginning: one dead, the other missing, the gun on the beach, the car, the boat, the girl . . . At any rate, Minns was right, Waddington was no killer, and if he had been he would hardly have been daft enough to go back for a second look three days later. But suppose David had shot his brother in a quarrel over the Waddington business then panicked and bolted?

Could it have been like that? Hardly. If Joseph was murdered he was shot while sitting at his desk with the gun held to his head. In other words, if he was murdered, it was in cold blood. Far more likely that Joseph shot himself. But his suicide would focus attention on the affairs of the antique shop and that would be unhealthy for David. But David had just had five thousand pounds' worth of coloured glass dropped in his lap. Had this been sufficient inducement for him to bring forward his plan to clear out?

What plan? With an elaborately prepared cover ready to move into he hadn't turned up there. Apparently he had not got that far. Add to that the cash and valuables left in the safe and the gun on the beach and it began to look more like panic flight than planned retreat. 'Which,' Wycliffe muttered to himself, 'is more or less where we came in.'

Yet against that shambles there was the car, astutely hidden, the note to set Toby Williams's mind at rest about *Manna* and the prints which had been removed in the downstairs office. Judicious foresight and panic bungling in about equal measure.

Quod est absurdum! as they used to say in the geometry books.

The telephone rang. 'Wycliffe.'

It was the harbour master, Sam Foster. 'It's possible we've got something for you, Mr Wycliffe.'

'About *Manna*?'

'Indirectly. Ron Bryce, the harbour master at Porthellin, rang me this morning about a dinghy they found holed and floating gunnel-down on Sunday morning. She was brought in and pulled up on the slipway there. This sort of thing happens all too often early in the season when the weather is dicey; dinghies break loose from their moorings or they may be washed off the beaches. Anyway, Ron didn't think much about it till this morning when he noticed a baling tin wedged under one of the thwarts and he saw the name, *Manna* sort of scratched on it. There are dozens of these little two metre dinghies about and one is much like another but the baling tin clinches it.'

Wycliffe thanked him. 'I'll get hold of Toby Williams and we'll go down together and take a look.'

But before leaving the office he telephoned Superintendent Redfern at Bournemouth.

'You seem very edgy about this one, Charles!' (Did it show even on the telephone?) 'Anyway, the girl spent the night at the flat and an hour ago she was still there; no sign of any man but she's been questioning the caretaker about Page. When did he last see Page? How long did he stay? The caretaker told our chap that Page had been there for a couple of nights a fortnight ago. That's all for now, but we'll keep in touch.'

Porthellin village lay three miles down the coast in a bay of the same name. Sheltered from the west and south by the crook of Laira Head, it lies more or less open to the south-east. Once the village lived off fish, now it is a tourist trap but April is too early for them.

Wycliffe picked up Toby Williams at St Juliot and drove over the hump of the peninsula through a maze of lanes which were becoming lush with spring growth. Toby sat immobile in the front passenger seat, staring straight ahead, smoking his pipe which had an incredibly short stem.

'Did you ever come across Major Parkyn when he had a boat at St Juliot?'

'The major? Yes, I looked after his boat for a couple of seasons. Nice little craft; cutter-rigged with auxiliary motor . . . The *Clarissa* – that's what she was called. Never forget the name of a boat . . . 'E sold 'er a couple of years back to a chap over to Brixham.'

'How did you get on with him?'

'All right. Never said much but never grumbled neither.'

'A good man with a boat?'

'Oh, the major knew 'ow to handle a boat. No doubt about that; he could take 'er out in most any weather and come back with a dry arse as they say.'

On the outskirts of Porthellin a sprawl of ugly bungalows gave way to the old stone cottages of the original village, then they were in the single main street which was so narrow that it was impossible for two vehicles to pass and traffic was regulated by lights. Now the village seemed deserted, the gift shops were closed and shuttered, cafés were boarded up and only a couple of food shops remained open to cope with the slender winter trade. The traffic lights flicked pointlessly through their routine. Ron Bryce, lanky and one-eyed, was waiting for them. His other eye was permanently closed on an empty socket. The tide was just beginning to make and there were patches of slimy mud still showing in the basin. The holed dinghy was drawn up on the slipway. Toby Williams looked her over.

'That's Mr Clement's dinghy all right. I can tell from the little split in the stern thwart.'

She was carvel built and the planking had been stove in amidships below the waterline.

Wycliffe said, 'Where was she picked up?'

Bryce pointed to a stretch of sandy beach beyond the village. 'Off Hucket's Cove there. She was riding gunnel under. Bert Simms spotted her and brought her in.

Sunday morning about twelve when the tide was three-parts in.'

Wycliffe picked up the end of the painter which was neatly whipped, there was no question of its having frayed through or having been cut.

Toby said. 'Mr Clement weren't the sort to lose 'is dinghy.'

The three men stood on the slipway contemplating the little craft, watched by several locals who were waiting outside the pub for the doors to open.

Wycliffe said, 'If he deliberately cast the dinghy adrift would he have gained much in either speed or the distance she would travel?'

Ron Bryce studied Wycliffe with his single eye. 'There could be something in that. Towing a dinghy even with a short line can be a drag though it don't usually signify much.'

Toby, better informed about the problem on Wycliffe's mind, came straight to the point. 'It wouldn't 've made five miles difference to 'er range and not 'alf a knot to 'er speed.' He lifted his yachtsman's cap and scratched his head. 'She must 've put in somewhere if only for fuel but why ain't we 'eard?'

The sky was clouding over as the wind rose off the sea in preparation for another squall.

'Where did *Manna* carry her name?'

Toby considered. 'On 'er transom an' on the front of the wheel-'ouse.'

'Easily changed?'

'If you 'ad new boards ready to put in place or if you 'ad time to re-paint 'em, but changing 'er name wouldn' account for the dinghy.'

'No, it wouldn't; I was trying to think of possibilities.'

The rain came hissing down, driven before the wind, and the three men hurried across to the pub which had just opened.

'Let's try again . . . ' Wycliffe had ordered drinks and

they were sitting round one of the painted metal tables at some distance from the bar. 'Say that Clement put out from St Juliot between two or three on Sunday morning, a couple of hours or less into the ebb. I understand that it was calm—'

Toby interrupted. 'Not all that calm – not outside Laira; there was a fresh breeze from the south-east, enough to bring up quite a chop – nothing to worry a boat like *Manna* but she would lose a bit if she was 'eading into it.'

'All right, it was choppy. Now, say that somewhere off here he abandoned *Manna* and took to the dinghy—'

The two men looked at him in amazement. 'Why would 'e do a damn fool thing like that?'

Excursions into lateral thinking are all very well until they run up against a wall of common sense. Why, indeed? 'But *if* he did, could he have made it ashore?'

Both men shook their heads. 'Not in the dinghy, not if he was outside. Not with the ebb and a choppy sea, he'd never have brought her in. Of course, if he was in the bay and inside the shelter of Laira, it would be different. He could've rowed himself ashore all right then.' It was Bryce speaking and he turned to Toby for confirmation.

Toby nodded. 'Yes, but it's a damn fool notion, Mr Wycliffe. I mean, if 'e brought the launch in under Laira then abandoned 'er, where is she?' He looked out of the window at the grey waste of sea, still lashed by rain, and said with heavy sarcasm, 'I don't see *Manna* out there, do you?'

Bryce grinned. 'Toby's right, Mr Wycliffe, she'd have gone ashore on the rocks next tide and probably ended up like the dinghy.'

But Wycliffe was not giving up. 'Just one more question. If the dinghy broke adrift or was cast adrift from her tow, outside the bay on an ebbing tide, would you expect her to end up in the bay the next morning?'

Bryce paused with his beer half-way to his lips. 'No, I

wouldn't. You got a point there, Mr Wycliffe. Almost for sure she'd have drifted further down the coast.'

Toby emptied his glass, looking troubled. 'Yes I go along with that.'

Wycliffe thought, Mr de Bono rides again! 'So it looks as though the launch probably did come into the bay and that the dinghy was set adrift in the bay – perhaps after someone came ashore in her.'

'And the *Manna*?' The question came from Toby.

'If there were two men, one might have gone ashore while the other put to sea again.'

Toby nodded. 'That could be, it's the only way to make sense of it all.'

Sense for Toby Williams but did it make sense for the case? Two men again. He arranged for Bryce to get the dinghy under cover in an old fish loft and for a search to be made along the shore for the oars, then the three of them had a meal in a little room behind the bar – grilled mackerel with boiled potatoes.

It was two o'clock when Wycliffe arrived back at his office. The morning's work had served to confuse him rather than otherwise. Two men, one of whom had gone ashore at Hucket's Cove. If one of the men was David Clement who was the other? And which of them had gone ashore?

While he was out there had been a call from a lawyer with offices in Bear Street; a lawyer he had never heard of, a certain Everett Friend. Friend had said that he had information about Joseph Clement's will and that he wanted to talk to someone concerned in the investigation of his death.

Plain speaking from any lawyer. Wycliffe decided to go himself.

Everett Friend was not prosperous, he had an office over the Bear Street bakery; two dingy little rooms and a landing cluttered with wooden filing cabinets like stacked coffins. In one of the rooms a middle-aged woman sat at a table with a pre-war Remington and a telephone; in the other Mr Friend brooded over a desk littered with dusty pocket files and bundles of paper tied with pink tape.

Friend belonged to Joseph's generation and he was a man of the same stamp; one could guess that they shared other characteristics including an innate gentleness which unsuited them for business. He greeted Wycliffe with a sad smile; wheezy-voiced, watery-eyed and smelling of menthol.

'I've been away from the office for a couple of days with a bad cold. I heard of poor Joseph's death yesterday but there was nothing I could do . . . My Clerk . . . ' He gestured vaguely towards the other room but did not finish his sentence.

'You said something about a will.'

Mr Friend stirred himself as far as to remove the tape from one of the pocket files. 'Yes, we have custody of his will. His father employed another solicitor but when Joseph took over he came to me. We were at school together . . . Do you really think that he was murdered, Superintendent?'

The lawyer's contribution was circumlocutory and lugubrious; fragments of information emerged unpredictably like droplets of moisture condensing out of a fog. Wycliffe sat back in his chair, put on his most bland expression and resigned himself. He was seated by a low window which overlooked the bakery yard and from time to time a stout lad in grey overalls crossed between the buildings carrying a sheath of cakes or rolls on his head – for all the world like a figure in a Brueghel painting.

Under the partnership agreement David received forty percent of the net profits and secured a similar interest in all other assets *except* the building. Friend leaned forward on his desk to emphasize the point. 'Except the building. It was as though Joe had some

101

uneasiness about the partnership even then for he kept the building in his own name.'

'The partnership was not a success?'

The lawyer took time off to blow his nose. 'Joe never confided in me but I certainly had the impression that it had been a great mistake and this was confirmed when he gave me instructions to prepare a new will . . . '

'About the will . . . '

But it was another five minutes before he succeeded in bringing Friend to the point. At last the lawyer took a single sheet of paper from the pocket file and read it through as though seeing it for the first time.

'Yes, this supersedes an earlier will made in favour of his brother, David. In this will, made less than a year ago, he leaves everything to his friend, Michael John Lane of St John's Court, and I am appointed executor.'

'Do you know this man Lane?'

'By sight. He's a cabinet maker and he has a workshop next to his house—'

'Married?'

'I think I'm right in saying that he is a bachelor as Joseph was.'

'Has he been notified?'

'I telephoned him this morning and I have an appointment with him tomorrow.'

'What about the funeral?'

Friend became even more solemn. 'Under the will I am required to make arrangements for the interment. It seems that Joseph had a horror of cremation. I have been in touch with the coroner's office and I should receive a disposal order this afternoon. As you know, the inquest stands adjourned. I have provisionally arranged for the funeral to take place at Mount Charles cemetery at three o'clock on Friday afternoon.'

Friend came with him to the top of the stairs where they were enveloped by the warm, yeasty smell of fresh bread.

'If Joseph was murdered, Superintendent, I hope that you will succeed in finding his killer. Joseph was an honest man and there are not too many of them left.'

Wycliffe walked the few yards to Annie's restaurant. She was at work with a vacuum cleaner and chairs were stacked on the tables. She switched off the cleaner and turned to him with a surprisingly girlish smile.

'I hope I did right yesterday.'

He was warm in his thanks. 'You shall have a personal letter from the chief constable to hang on the wall.'

She laughed, 'It would scare my customers away.'

'Do you know a friend of Joseph called Michael Lane?'

'Lane? The only Lane I know round here is Bunny Lane, the cabinet maker. Everybody calls him Bunny because he's got a hare-lip. I didn't know he was a friend of Joseph but he could have been.'

'Married?'

'No, he's a bachelor and he's lived alone since his mother died. Come to think of it he and Joseph would have a lot in common.'

St John's Court was tucked away behind Bear Street at the harbour end; a little square of houses. Bunny Lane's was like all the others except for the workshop attached, a sensible arrangement which, remarkably, had survived the planners. The door of the workshop was open and Wycliffe went in, his nostrils assailed by the scent of freshly worked timber and glue. It was a shed, long and dimly lit by windows of overlapping panes of glass. There was a central bench on which a number of hardwood drawers were held in clamps to allow the glue to set; pieces of reproduction period furniture stood about at random and in all stages of completion and there were sophisticated machines for drilling, planing and sawing.

'Anybody home?'

A short, stocky man with dark curly hair came out of a sort of glass cage where an electric lamp burned. He had a generous moustache which just failed to cover his hare-lip and when he spoke his words came with a sibilant whistle.

'Superintendent Wycliffe.'

'I suppose you've come about Joe; you'd better come into the house.'

Wycliffe followed him out to a back-yard, through a lean-to greenhouse with a giant vine, through a workman-like kitchen and into a plain but clean and comfortable living-room. There was an open grate, a cast-iron crock for coal, three leather armchairs, fibre matting on the floor, a big square table and a number of kitchen chairs. On the mantelpiece an alarm clock ticked loudly. No sign of period furniture either genuine or reproduction. On the walls were tiers of shelves crammed with books, many of them without spines and therefore anonymous.

Lane said, 'I've got a little parlour but I never use it – not since my mother died.'

'Obviously you've heard what happened to your friend Joseph.'

Lane nodded. He was very dark with rather sombre eyes and a heavy set to his jaw which gave an impression of strength.

'You didn't think to contact us?'

'What good would it have done?' He was not aggressive, merely objective.

'You were close friends?'

'I suppose you could say that, I've never thought about it. Joe's been coming here two or three times a week for several years.'

Wycliffe was looking round, wondering how the two men spent their time, then it dawned on him that this was where Parkyn and Joseph met, not two men but three gathered round the fire in this room which reminded him of the farm kitchen of his childhood; one of the three armchairs was the major's.

'You haven't mentioned Parkyn.'

'You didn't ask about him.'

'But the three of you met here regularly?'

'There's no secret about it.'

No secret, certainly, but Wycliffe was beginning to understand; in meeting as they did the three men retained their own individuality, their own privacy. There was no commitment, nothing was surrendered, and none felt free to speak of the others. Parkyn had not mentioned Lane and Lane had not referred to Parkyn.

'Just the three of you?'

Lane smiled briefly, revealing more of his hare-lip, 'Just the three of us.'

'How did you spend your time?'

The question arose from curiosity more than anything else and Lane did not resent it.

'It depends; sometimes we sit and talk, sometimes we just sit. There's always a glass and a smoke, and sometimes we play dominoes.' He glanced across at the big square table covered with oilcloth.

Wycliffe could see the attraction of this way of going on. If he was ever alone it was the kind of relationship he might seek. He asked, knowing the answer in advance, 'Did Clement confide in you at all?'

Lane shook his head, 'It wasn't like that.'

'I imagine you are as anxious to find out who killed him – if he didn't die by his own hand – as we are.'

'There shouldn't be much difficulty about that; David has cleared out, hasn't he?'

Exactly Parkyn's response if not his actual words.

'Was there friction between the brothers?'

Lane looked at him appraisingly and seemed to reach a decision. 'I won't be a minute.' He disappeared into the kitchen and came back with a bottle of white wine and two glasses.

'Will you try it? It's three years old and made from my

105

own grapes mostly.' He drew the cork and poured a little of the wine into a glass. 'Try it – see if you like it.'

It was good – light and flowery. Lane filled the glasses.

'Your good health!' A moment or two for appreciation then, 'Does Parkyn drink wine when he's here?'

Lane was curt. 'The major drinks whatever he feels like drinking at the time. But you were asking about Joseph and his brother.' He sipped his wine then wiped his moustache with a khaki-coloured handkerchief. 'Joseph was a simple sort of chap really – not stupid by any means, but straightforward. When his father died he was quite capable of carrying on the business as it always had been and that is what he did. It was only when the prodigal son returned that Joe got into difficulties. He wasn't up to his brother's tricks, he just didn't understand that sort and almost before he knew it he was up to his eyes in all sorts of funny business.'

Lane lifted his glass to the light, admiring the clarity and colour of his wine. 'Nice, isn't it? Makes you feel good to look at it.' Then he sighed. 'It's hard to believe that they were brothers, they were as different as chalk and cheese.'

'Did Joseph know what his brother was up to?'

'I don't know what he knew; all I can say is that he was a very worried man. For more than a year he hasn't been himself.'

'But he never discussed his troubles with you?'

'No. He would make the odd remark like, "I don't know where it will all end," or "One of these days he will land us both in trouble." Things like that but no details.' Lane fingered his glass. 'We didn't pry into each other's affairs, we didn't ask questions or offer advice.'

It wasn't difficult to imagine the three of them, sitting round the fire in the leather armchairs, a bottle of wine and a bottle of whisky close at hand; saying little, making no demands and so able to relax in each other's company. Had one of them wanted a closer relationship no doubt he would have married.

'Did you know that he was leaving everything to you?'

'Not until the lawyer phoned; it was very thoughtful of him.'

'You say that the three of you met here two or three times a week; did you never go to Parkyn's place or to the shop?'

Lane's reproachful look seemed to suggest that he thought Wycliffe had understood the situation better but he contented himself with a simple, 'No.'

'You never visted the shop?'

'Sometimes on business. I did small repair jobs and a certain amount of restoration work for them. That's how I first met Joseph – back in his father's time. They made a big thing of furniture then, and when they had a nice piece that needed a bit of attention they sent for me.'

'And recently?'

He shrugged. 'I've probably been in the shop five or six times in the past two years.'

'And when was the last time?'

'Saturday night – I didn't actually go in but I called there.'

Wycliffe felt a little tremor of excitement. 'Last Saturday night – at what time?'

'A bit before ten, a quarter to, maybe. I don't know exactly. It was pure chance. When Joe was here on Thursday evening I offered to lend him Anthony Coleridge's book on Chippendale but he forgot to take it. On Saturday I'd been cooped up in the workshop all day so in the evening, when the rain stopped, I thought I'd take a stroll and it occurred to me to drop the book in.'

'You went to the side-door?'

'I intended to but I saw a light in the back of the shop so I just tapped on the glass and David came out.'

'Did you see Joseph?'

'No, David said that he was a bit seedy and that he'd gone to bed so I gave David the book and asked him to pass it on.'

'You realize that must have been somewhere near the time Joseph died?'

'I don't know when Joseph died. I only know what I read in the newspaper.'

'In any case, you were the last person we know of to see David Clement. How did he seem? Normal? Excited? Edgy?'

Lane laughed briefly. 'Much as usual – not exactly welcoming and I had the impression that he was expecting someone else but I could be wrong about that.'

Wycliffe stood up. 'Thanks for the wine.'

Lane saw him out by the front door into a deserted square which looked like a film set waiting for the action to begin. He collected his car and drove back to his office feeling subdued. The visit had left a vivid impression on his mind; he could see the three men seated round the hearth in Lane's living-room, each with a glass in his hand, staring at the fire. For long periods the silence would be broken only by the ticking of the clock on the mantelpiece and the occasional sounds of coals settling in the grate. The atmosphere would be close with a thin pall of smoke drifting near the ceiling and the fruity smell of the wine blending with the more astringent odour of the major's whisky.

'Shall I top you up, Joe?'

'No, thanks; I'm well enough.'

Lane would pour a little of the clear pale wine into his own glass then place the bottle well away from the fire to keep it cool. The clock would tick away another five, ten – perhaps fifteen minutes . . . The major would say, 'Do you think a game . . . ?' And they would move to the square table taking their glasses with them. The rattle of dominoes, the draw, the play . . .

'Your glass is empty, Major. Try a drop of this for a change . . .'

Did they call the major Gavin? It was unlikely.

A sort of refuge. For the major from his sister, her house, and possibly from disillusionment. For Clement, from his brother and from the business which had been his standby and was now only a source of worry and foreboding. For Lane – perhaps from his hare-lip and all that it had meant to him since infancy when he had first realized that he was different.

Kersey was waiting for Wycliffe.

'Mr Redfern telephoned. Molly Stokes caught the eleven o'clock train and she arrived at three. I've put Fowler to keep an eye on her. According to Mr Redfern she made no contacts that could mean anything and he thinks she's as anxious to find Clement as we are.'

'What about the Waddington saga?'

'Bourne is looking after Sergeant Minns. Minns has had two sessions with Waddington, with a lawyer, and he's spoken to his chief on the phone. They want him back in London.'

Wycliffe's mind was still on Lane and the meetings of the three men in his living-room. To Kersey he must have seemed heavy and inattentive.

'What do you think?'

Kersey said, 'I can't see Waddington as a killer.'

'Neither can I and if we want him we shall know where to find him. Tell Bourne to make sure he gets the paperwork right and when it's done they can have him.'

Wycliffe always found it difficult to sustain a logical train of thought for long. His mind didn't work that way. Ideas seemed to surface, link together in some sort of pattern and break up again as in a kaleidoscope which is gently shaken. Now and then a particular pattern appealed to him and he would try to look at it more closely.

'Perhaps we are meant to think that David Clement has cleared out.'

'You mean that he hasn't?'

'That's the other side of the coin and it scarcely makes sense, does it?'

Kersey tried again. 'You mean that he might still be here in the city?'

'That doesn't seem very likely.'

'No, I don't think it does.'

Wycliffe had arrived at a decision. 'Are you doing anything special this evening?'

Kersey grinned. His family didn't go in for much social life. 'I think we might have a free evening.'

'I want you to go to Bournemouth – clear it with Mr Redfern first – and see what you can find out about this Alan Page, the chap who holds the lease on the flat in Canning Terrace. We must be sure that he is Clement, otherwise we shall be caught with egg on our faces. If he is, then we want to know everything about him as Page.'

'Anything else, sir?'

'No. I'm going to talk to Molly Stokes.'

But before he could get away he had to cope with Diane at her most efficient.

'Mr Bellings is wondering if you've overlooked his memo 395/TC.'

'What's it about?'

'Your views on the possibility of cutting fuel costs by re-planning the rosters of crime and traffic mobiles.'

'The answer is yes.'

'Yes, what?'

'I have overlooked it.'

Diane would have liked to push a little harder but thought better of it. 'Then there's the crime prevention advertising campaign on TV. The agency have the specimen runs ready and the chief would like to see them with you.'

'When?'

'Tomorrow at ten.'

'That's another day.'

It was childish. He was childish; but there was more to it than that. Sometimes he felt the need to cut himself off from everything that was not connected with the case on hand, otherwise he would lose touch; ideas would not surface and patterns would refuse to form.

It was gone six when he eventually arrived in Bear Street and parked by the police caravan. The wind had dropped but the sky was still heavy with rain clouds. The shops were shut and the street was empty. He did not go into the van but walked along the wharf looking down at the still, sombre waters of the harbour.

If Clement had really bolted, surely he would have gone to Bournemouth, to the flat. But *Manna* had been taken from her moorings and her dinghy had turned up, damaged, off Hucket's Cove. Somebody had gone ashore there, of that he felt certain. But had there been one man on the launch or two? David Clement alone, or David Clement and another? If two, then one had remained on board the launch and taken her – where? But if Clement was alone, what had happened to *Manna*? Had he scuttled her? The idea came to mind only to be dismissed. He was muttering to himself. Drops of rain made tremulous expanding circles on the surface of the water; a gull, perched on the roof of the police van, fixed him with a sardonic eye.

And where did Lane come in? And Parkyn? Did they come in at all? The major, Bunny and Joe. Like a circus act. The three musketeers. All for each and each for all. Lane admitted being at the shop at shortly before ten; the major knew all about boats and it was his gun though probably stolen. And Joe was dead.

Joe was dead. And David was missing.

Time to stop this nonsense! Wycliffe rebuked himself. It was starting to rain much harder and he pulled up the collar of his mackintosh and set off to call on Molly Stokes. Fowler was on duty in Godolphin Street in the not very original cover of a television repair van. It faced

111

away from the house but, presumably, he could see what went on through his wing mirror.

He rang the bell of the girl's flat and after a short wait the door was opened on a chain.

'Oh, it's you! What do you want now?'

She released the chain and opened the door wide. She wore a housecoat of dark, silky material with an oriental design which, with her almost black hair, was in startling contrast with the pallor of her face. She looked ill and it was obvious that she was a very worried young woman.

'You'd better come in, I suppose.'

The little flat was filled with a not very appetizing smell of cooking; the kitchen door was open and he could see saucepans on the stove.

'Will you be long? If so I'd better turn that off.'

'It depends on you.'

She whisked into the kitchen, turned off the stove, and came back, closing the door behind her. 'Sit down if you want to.'

But he continued to stand while she perched on the arm of one of the chairs and lit a cigarette. He was in no hurry to begin.

'Well?'

'You've been away.'

'Have I?'

'Bournemouth, wasn't it?'

'Is that illegal?'

'Why did you go?'

She was watching him closely; no fool, she knew better than to lie outright. 'I do sometimes on my change-over break at the hospital.'

'Did you stay with friends?'

She hesitated. 'Not exactly.'

'Flat C on the fourth floor of Gort House.'

She was shaken but she made an effort to come back

112

fighting. 'I don't suppose I can stop you spying on me but I don't know what good it will do you.'

'Is Alan Page your friend?'

She did not answer. The gas fire was burning and to Wycliffe, in his heavy mackintosh, it seemed uncomfortably hot but she was wearing little or nothing under her housecoat.

'Did you meet Page?'

'No.' She fetched an ornament from the mantelpiece to use as an ashtray.

'Where is he?

'I've no idea at the moment; he sells jewellery and fancy goods to the shops and he travels a lot.'

'But you have a key to his flat.'

'Yes.'

'What does Clement think about that?'

'That is none of your business.'

'At this moment one of my officers is on his way to Bournemouth to investigate the myth of Page.'

It was not in his nature to bully a witness but, without realizing it, he had been standing over the girl and his manner probably seemed menacing. At any rate there was a flicker of alarm in her eyes.

He went on, less dramatically. 'He will confirm that Alan Page and David Clement are the same and then we shall know that the flat and the alias were intended to help Clement get out from under whenever things got too rough for him. I'm not really very concerned with Clement the thief, but I am very concerned with Clement, the possible murderer.'

She held her ground and said in a level voice. 'I've no more idea than you have where David is; you can believe that or not – as you wish, but, as I've told you before, he is no killer.'

'But you went to Bournemouth expecting – at least hoping, to meet him?'

She did not answer but he had no need of an answer. He took off his mackintosh and laid it across one of the chairs then he sat down. It was a gesture, an acknowledgement that in some sense they had come to terms.

'For two years at least David Clement had been mixed up with a London mob. He's been responsible for organizing break-ins and for disposing of stolen property through his business connections in the antiques trade. In that time he must have accumulated a considerable sum of money; do you imagine for one moment that this money has gone into Clement Brothers Antiques Limited?'

She tapped the ash from her cigarette. 'Is this some sort of quiz? I've told you, I know nothing of David's business affairs.'

'It's an old trick to prepare for retirement from a venture in crime by establishing another identity – someone to hold the purse while the fight is on. It's less common than it was because professional snoopers and the computer make it more difficult but it can still be done. It's one of the freedoms we can still enjoy if we're smart enough.'

She swept back her dark hair with a careless movement of her arm. She really was an attractive girl, and a shrewd one. 'Why are you saying all this to me?'

'Would you have known about Clement's other life if you weren't intended to share it one day? Would you have agreed to share it unless it offered you something a good deal better than you have at the moment? You are no starry-eyed young girl, head-over-heels in love and blind to the grocery bills.'

She stubbed out her cigarette. 'Thanks for the testimonial but where does it all lead?'

'Simply to this: if Clement hasn't turned up in his new role he must have been prevented by something important. I want to know what that something is and so do you.'

She said nothing though he sensed that she was tempted.

'*Manna*'s dinghy has been found off Hucket's Cove in Porthellin Bay.'

That startled her. 'Wrecked?'

'Damaged; it looks as though someone came ashore in her then set her adrift. She was found on Sunday morning but I've only just heard of it.'

She was caught off guard. 'You think that he might—' But whatever it was she had been going to say she changed her mind.

It seemed the moment to go.

He went downstairs and out into the street. Fowler had turned the van round to get better vision as the light faded. At least he had something to put in his report to show that he had stayed awake. The rain was falling vertically and Wycliffe quickened his pace along Godolphin Street and through Bear Street to the old harbour and the police van.

D.C. Richards was duty officer and Dixon was there typing house-to-house reports. Poor old Richards suffered from premature hardening of the intellectual arteries. He was morbidly conscientious and totally lacking in imagination.

'Anything new?'

Richards shook his head. 'It's dead, sir; in my opinion we're wasting our time here.'

'Is the house-to-house complete?'

Richards nodded towards Dixon. 'Dixon is typing his last report.'

'All right, we'll move the van tomorrow and you can tell them to cancel the roster from then.'

This upset Richards who liked to grumble but did not really want to be taken notice of because that involved responsibility. 'I didn't want to speak out of turn, sir.'

'No question of that. You said what you thought and you are probably right.'

He looked round the little compartment, reluctant to tear himself away and go home. Last Sunday he had never heard of the Clement brothers, of Major Parkyn or of Bunny Lane; now it seemed that his life was bound up with theirs and it was a wrench to walk out on them and return to his own domestic circle. He stood over Dixon, fingering the sheets and putting the young man off so that he fumbled the keys.

'These are the last four, sir. We managed most of the street yesterday but there are always a few out, or away. I think the second one might be worth following up.'

Dixon made one more desperate attempt to finish and then drew out the sheets with a flourish. 'I'll just separate the carbons . . . ' He did so, then handed a sheet from the pile over to Wycliffe.

Wycliffe glanced at the report. 'Who's Marilyn Ford?'

There was a dry cackle from Richards and Dixon said, 'She's a pro, sir. She and another girl have rooms over the fish shop which is next to Annie Blazek's place and almost opposite the antique shop. There is a little passage beside the fish shop and the girls have their own entrance up a flight of steps. They both went off to what they call, "an engagement in the country" and they didn't get back until this morning. That's why we haven't been in touch with this girl before.'

'All right. Let's have it.'

'Well, Marilyn says that she was in her room alone; a client had just left, and she heard a sort of bang – like a car backfiring but she hadn't heard any cars in the street. She looked out of her window but she couldn't see anything and she forgot about it.'

'This, I take it, was Saturday evening?'

'Yes, shortly after nine. She remembered the bang when I started talking about a shot.'

'You think she's reliable?'

Dixon frowned. 'You know what these girls are, sir. When they've got no reason to lie they make good

116

witnesses; they've got to have their wits about them or they wouldn't last long. More than that, they don't want to upset our lot if they can help it.'

If the girl really had heard a shot shortly after nine o'clock then that seemed to let brother David out, for at that time he was at the *Seven Stars* buying his cigarettes.

There was another report from the man who had interviewed the landlady of the *Unicorn* where Waddington had stayed. According to her, Waddington had arrived there between half-past eight and nine which provided him with an alibi if he needed one.

Enough hinged on the prostitute's evidence to warrant checking. It might be necessary to arrange an action replay with someone firing the gun in Joseph's room to find out what could be heard in the girl's flat.

He walked up Bear Street as far as the fish shop. It was still raining and there were few people about. The windows of Annie's restaurant were steamed over so that it was impossible to see inside. The narrow passage by the fish shop led to a yard and from the yard there was a flight of steps to the first floor. At the top of the steps there was a covered landing, a light and a front door with two bells, one of which was labelled M. Ford. Wycliffe pressed the bell and hoped that the girl was free.

The door was opened almost at once by a plump brunette.

'Miss Ford.'

'That's me.'

The Monro legend had persuded him that all Marilyns were blonde but here was proof to the contrary. She wore a pale pink wrap-over-dress and she had dark, laughing eyes. Over the years he had had dealings with many prostitutes but he had known very few who really laughed. This girl seemed to be on the point of laughing all the time.

'Police. Superintendent Wycliffe.'

'You'd better come in.'

Her room, which overlooked the street, gave one the impression that a candy-floss machine had got the bit between its teeth and bolted. It was dimly lit and there were cushions and draperies in pastel shades everywhere. The smell was like a close encounter with the cosmetics department of a big store and he felt that he was being enmeshed in scented cotton wool. He stood in the middle of the room like the proverbial bull in a china shop with his mackintosh dripping on the carpet.

'I suppose it's about the shot.' She was a little unsure how to treat him. 'There isn't any more I can tell you. I had a visitor who left a few minutes before nine and this bang came not long afterwards. I remember it was after the church clock struck.'

'So you would be prepared to swear if necessary that it was after nine o'clock?'

She nodded vigorously. 'Oh, yes. Definitely.'

He asked her one or two more questions for form's sake, standing by the window, looking down into the street. The street was empty and the streaming road surface shone in the light of the street lamps. A couple, sharing an umbrella, came into sight and made for Annie's next door. Opposite, the antique shop already had that derelict look which buildings have when they are waiting for the 'For Sale' notices to go up.

'I don't suppose you saw anyone entering or leaving the antique shop that evening?'

'No – no, I didn't . . . ' She paused. 'Wait a minute, I've been in the country for a couple of days and it puts things out of your head – there was somebody, I remember now. I should think it was a bit before ten. I went to the window to look down into the street like you do sometimes if you're a bit bored. There was nobody about, then I saw a man coming up the street from the harbour end. He was on the same side as the antique shop and when he got there he went to the shop door and I think he must have tapped on the glass or something because somebody came and let him in.'

'You're quite sure about this?'

'Yes, I am. I'd forgotten but you know how things come back to you.'

'You know the Clement brothers, I suppose?'

'By sight, yes.'

'So it wasn't one of them you saw?'

'Oh, no. Definitely not. I couldn't see this man all that well but well enough for that. He wasn't very tall but broad and he wore a cloth cap – not many men do these days so I noticed.'

As Wycliffe's eyes became accustomed to the dim light he saw the bed which seemed to be a mound of pink silk. Marilyn must have a good class clientele; no short-time customers for her.

'Could you see who it was let the man in?'

'No, they didn't switch the lights on.'

'Do you know a man called Bunny Lane – a man with a hare-lip?'

She shook her head. 'I can't say I do. Is he from round here?'

She was beginning to show signs of edginess, once or twice she glanced at her watch; evidently she was expecting a client and wanted him to go. Finally she took her courage in both hands: 'Look, I'm sorry . . . I'm expecting a friend . . . '

As he reached the bottom of the stairs he heard footsteps coming, not from Bear Street but from the back of the premises. A man emerged from the darkness and hesitated when he saw Wycliffe. Some of Marilyn's friends preferred the back way in.

The girl's description fitted Bunny Lane as far as it went and it seemed likely he might wear a cloth cap. Bunny had said that he had called at the shop with a book for Joseph but he was quite definite that he had not gone in.

Wycliffe drove home. Helen heard the car and was standing in the doorway of the house from which light streamed out across the gravel. It was still raining hard.

'Aren't you glad you took your heavy raincoat?'

CHAPTER SIX

The alarm buzzed insistently and he reached out to stifle it. He was aggressively disposed to alarms of all sorts but most of all to the modern buzzers, hooters, sirens and other banshee devices. What was wrong with bells?

'Was that the alarm?'

'Yes.'

Helen sighed. 'Pity! I was hoping I'd dreamt it.' She turned over on her back and wriggled luxuriously. 'You haven't forgotten that Ruth is coming home today?'

He had but he wasn't going to admit it. Ruth was their daughter, aged twenty-three.

'She's due around lunchtime. I suppose there's no chance of you taking the afternoon off?'

'None I'm afraid.'

'But you'll make it in time for a meal at a reasonable hour this evening?'

'I'll try.'

'If you don't I'll file for divorce. Do you know we haven't seen her for six months?'

'She's happy in her job.'

'She seems to be but sometimes I think there's more to it than that.'

'Such as?'

'That it's more her boss than her job.'

'Ah well, he's rich.'

'Charles! When you say things like that you worry me. I'm not altogether sure that you're joking.'

'Neither am I. After all you wouldn't want her to start married life scraping the bottom of the barrel every month as we did.'

'I don't know. I never complained, did I?'

'No, but you had me.'

Another wet day; white horses in the estuary which meant that the wind had freshened again from the south or south-west. He arrived at the office by eight-thirty and already there were two reports on his desk. One was the forensic report on David Clement's car and told him nothing he did not already know except that they had found very small quantities of hardwood dust – probably oak – on the floor of the car by the driver's seat. It was tempting to think of Bunny Lane's workshop which was carpeted with the stuff but that would be too easy.

No news of *Manna* which was odd and getting odder day by day. A thirty-foot cabin cruiser doesn't just vanish off the face of the sea and such boats are largely portbound. When they put into shore they need a berth, they can't be dragged up on some secluded beach; they need fuel, they need water . . .

He picked up the telephone and asked to be put through to the harbour master.

'Mr Foster? . . . Wycliffe . . . Are you likely to be available in your office during the next hour? . . . Will it be convenient if I come along for a chat? . . . Thanks, I'll be there in fifteen minutes . . . '

It was an over-optimistic estimate; the traffic through the city centre on a wet morning seemed always on the point of coming to a permanent halt. He swore like anybody else and asked, 'Don't we have traffic policemen any more?'

Foster's office stood on the wharf by the 'new' harbour, next to the 'new' custom-house built in 1875. Wycliffe was ten minutes late but Foster, like most men of the sea, was leisurely and relaxed. He was a small man with a very red face which shone as though it had been polished.

'I suppose you have charts of the waters round here?'

'Of the estuary and the approaches.'

'Porthellin Bay?'

For answer Foster opened a long drawer and drew out an Admiralty chart which he laid on the desk. Wycliffe put his finger on a shallow indentation in the outline of Laira Head, a little to the south-west of the village.

'Hucket's Cove?'

Foster nodded. 'I gather the dinghy was found drifting just off there.'

'Yes. Now, perhaps you will treat what I'm going to ask you as confidential. It's a shot in the dark and will probably lead to nothing.'

'I'm not a great talker, Mr Wycliffe.'

'Good! Then my question is this; if I was in Porthellin Bay on the night of Saturday/Sunday in a motor cruiser which I wanted to scuttle then row myself ashore in the dinghy, how would I set about it? You can assume that I am a knowledgeable yachtsman, familiar with the coast.'

Foster's face registered amazement. 'Good God! You can't think – No, I won't ask questions, I'll see if it's possible to answer yours.' He took off his uniform cap and laid it aside, revealing a bald head which shone to match his face, then he settled to a careful study of the chart. At one point he consulted a little book with ruled columns in which entries had been made in ink. After a full ten minutes he turned to Wycliffe with a half-smile.

'It's an interesting problem. At first I thought there wasn't much prospect of giving you anything like a helpful answer; now I'm not so sure. I take it you want to scuttle several thousand pounds' worth of boat where it would be unlikely to be found in a hurry and then get ashore in the dinghy without too much risk of having to swim for it.'

Wycliffe nodded. 'That's about it.'

'Well, it happens that there are a number of factors limiting your choice – more than I thought. First, on the night in question, the wind was from the south-east –

force five to six on the Beaufort Scale, and that would be blowing straight into the bay. It would raise a bit of a sea and there would be some white water. While that wouldn't worry the launch, it would the dinghy – unless he took advantage of the shelter of Laira.'

With a soft pencil he ruled a faint line on the chart from the tip of Laira Head to the jetty at Porthellin. 'If I wanted to put myself ashore in the dinghy with an ebbing tide and a twenty-knot wind I'd want to be inside that line, for a start.'

Wycliffe looked at the roughly triangular area enclosed by the crooked headland and Foster's pencilled line. 'That leaves quite a lot of water.'

'Yes it does, but we can do better than that. If you didn't want your boat sticking up like a sore thumb at the first low-tide she would have to be well outside the low-water mark of the springs.' He sketched another pencil line. 'I don't think she could afford to be closer in than that. And there's another thing which should occur to anybody who knows the bay well, all this here . . . ' He shaded a substantial area extending out from the shore across the angle of Laira. 'All that is deep enough to cover your boat at any tide but the bottom is rocky and she might well break up in the first real easterly or south-easterly blow that coincided with a low tide. Then you'd have flotsam coming ashore in no time.'

He paused, smoothing his bald head and staring at the chart. 'It comes to this, then . . . ' He pencilled in an oval area lying off the cove. 'Here you have a pebbly bottom covered by four or five fathom at the average ebb – more at the neaps, less at the springs. If you were as knowledge-able as you say, and wanted to do such a damn-fool thing, you'd have done it inside that oval.'

'Roughly, how big an area is that?'

Foster laid a scale across the chart. 'Say four hundred yards long and about half that across.'

'Possible to search?'

He shrugged. 'I should think so; it would be a slow job. You'd need to quarter it with a boat towing a grapnel or a special trawl. That way you would pin-point the boat if she was there. After that it would be up to the divers.'

Foster replaced his cap with a pleased grin on his face. 'Only one thing, Mr Wycliffe, if you're going to use that I'd like a chance to check my facts first.'

Wycliffe drove back to headquarters not at all sure that he wasn't about to make a fool of himself but determined to go ahead unless they had news of *Manna* or of Clement. He was acting on a hunch but there was a kind of logic to support him. He could not believe that David Clement had gone off voluntarily leaving money and valuables in the safe. The alternative seemed to be that he had been kidnapped or even killed. If Clement had been killed then there was a body to dispose of and the scuttling of *Manna* would then appear in a new light.

'The chief wants to see you, Mr Wycliffe.' Something had occurred to disturb Diane's customary serenity, she looked almost distressed.

'Is he free now?'

'He said, whenever you came in.'

The chief constable and the deputy had their offices at the end of a carpeted corridor approached through a heavy panelled and padded door which closed with a swish of displaced air. The chief's personal assistant, a grey-haired lady of impressive dignity, known irreverently as Queenie said, 'I'll see if Mr Oldroyd is free.'

She pressed a button on the intercom. 'Mr Wycliffe is here, Mr Oldroyd.'

'Ask him to come in.'

Unlike Bellings, Oldroyd was, in Wycliffe's opinion, a real policeman, deeply concerned about crime and not merely about the statistics of crime. Wycliffe sometimes differed from his chief but with mutual understanding and that was more than could be said of his relations with the deputy.

Oldroyd was standing, looking out of the window at the rain-swept car park. 'Come in, Charles! Sit you down. Busy?'

'Yes.'

'The Clement affair. I've been reading the reports. Odd business, isn't it?'

Oldroyd was a spare figure, always casually dressed; like a country gentleman who has looked in at the estate office on his way to something more interesting. It was a deceptive impression; he was a professional to his fingertips. He turned from the window and sat in an armchair opposite Wycliffe.

'Too busy for crime prevention, I gather.'

'Frankly, sir, too busy for publicity stunts.'

Oldroyd sighed. 'I wish I was, but these things have to be done. In the long run we work with public approval or we don't work at all.'

'I suppose so.'

'You don't suppose anything of the sort.' Oldroyd laughed. 'You're arrogant, Charles, beneath that veneer of modesty. As long as you know you're right, what the hell does it matter what anybody else thinks?'

Wycliffe said nothing. The chief brought out a box of cigars. 'I don't suppose I can tempt you? All right, smoke that pipe of yours if you must.' He nipped off the end of a cigar and lit it. 'I don't suppose Bellings has told you his news?'

'News?'

'He's leaving us – off to Oxford, a lectureship in criminology. Don't talk about it until he tells you himself. A surprise, isn't it? I shall miss him. He helps to keep me on the administrative rails – you too, I shouldn't wonder.'

'He's a good adminstrator.'

Oldroyd smiled. 'We have to find someone to take his place. Of course there will be a Board but I shall have to work with the new man so I expect they will listen to me.'

Wycliffe was at sea, and looked it.

'I'm asking you, Charles, whether you would like to put yourself up for the job?'

'*Me?*'

'Why not? You've got the rank and the experience and God knows you've been critical enough of those of us who are in the hotter seats. It seems only fair that you should have a go.'

'It's not my line of country.'

Oldroyd drew on his cigar and released a thin spiral of blue-grey smoke. 'I know you want to keep the mud on your boots but you can't expect the top jobs to be done as you want them done unless your kind of people have the doing of them.'

'It's good of you to have me in mind and I appreciate it but—'

'Think it over, Charles; talk to Helen about it. It's Thursday – let's say next Wednesday evening. Come and have a meal with us – both of you and we can talk over what you decide.'

'Yes, of course. Thank you.'

He stood up to go.

'Don't be in such a hurry, Charles! This case – the Clement affair – Bellings is afraid you might get your fingers burnt dealing with Parkyn.'

'I'm not sure that it's my fingers he's worried about.'

A disapproving frown from the chief who liked his version of the proprieties to be observed. 'Your fingers, his fingers, my fingers – we are in it together, Charles! This is no one-man band.' Acid.

'Sorry.'

'Have you any reason to think that Parkyn might be involved – criminally involved, I mean?'

Wycliffe considered. 'He was on fairly intimate terms

with the dead man and he thinks that the younger brother was involved in the break-in at the house in Garrison Drive. A gun was stolen at that time and a bullet from that gun killed Joseph Clement.'

'Put like that it sounds pretty damning.'

'Yes, but there are other ways of putting it. The real answer is that I've got an open mind.'

'You've questioned him – how many times?'

'Twice, and I intend to see him again tonight.'

'Has he shown any resentment?'

'Not a bit. I get the impression that it amuses him.'

'Good! I just want to know where we stand. Go ahead. If there is any attempt at tail twisting you can rely on me to see 'em off.'

Wycliffe was at the door.

'Don't forget, Charles. Next Wednesday.'

Back in his office he felt slightly dazed. Diane put a fresh cup of coffee on his desk.

'You missed your coffee. I made some more.'

It dawned on him that he was being fussed over because he was supposed to have been on the carpet.

'Nothing from Mr Kersey?'

'No, Mr Wycliffe.'

He asked for the keys of the antique shop to be sent up to him. He could not have explained why he wanted to go there again; there was nothing he wanted to see, no new idea to be tried out. All he knew was that he must keep in touch. That was why he found it impossible to conduct an investigation from a desk, sending people here and there, issuing instructions and receiving reports. A little time away from the place where it happened, from the people most closely concerned, and he would begin to lose contact, to see people and places, not as they really were but as his mind had made them.

'Will you be back before lunch?'

'No, I shouldn't think so.'

He walked down the stairs and out of the building, ignoring the man at the desk, preoccupied, but not with thoughts of promotion. He was trying to justify to himself an expensive operation which might turn out to be a mare's nest. The hire of the launch . . . divers . . . two or three days, perhaps a week if the weather was bad. He drove through the city centre to Bear Street and parked outside the old custom-house. The police van had gone.

He walked along the street which was as busy as he had ever seen it; the pavements crowded and the traffic trying to edge its way through. One of the current Bear Street wrangles concerned the pros and cons of making it a pedestrian precinct. The rain had stopped and there was a blue sky just visible through a rift in the clouds.

He let himself into the antique shop by the side-door and climbed the stairs to the flat above. The rooms had already acquired a musty smell. He drew back the red velvet curtains in the living-room, letting in the light of day, and stood for a while looking down into the street.

Annie was having her quiet spell between coffee and lunch. He could see her putting pepper and salt pots on the tables and straightening the straw-bottomed chairs. Next door was the fishmongers with a colourful display of lobsters and crabs holding pride of place on the marble slab. On the floor above, Marilyn Ford's room was discreetly curtained. It was from that room with its candy-floss decor that she had looked down the rain-washed street and seen a man coming from the direction of the harbour – 'not very tall, but broad', and he wore a cloth cap. According to Marilyn it was a little before ten.

Bunny Lane had said, 'I'd been cooped up in the workshop all day so in the evening, when the rain had stopped, I thought I'd take a stroll and it occurred to me to drop the book in . . . I gave David the book and asked him to pass it on . . . '

The girl's story was different: ' . . . he went to the shop

door and I think he must have tapped on the glass or something because somebody came and opened the door and let him in.'

He turned back to the room and ran his eyes over the bookshelves and the piles of magazines and catalogues which littered the floor beneath the shelves. They were not all concerned with antiques, there were several yachting and power-boat magazines and in the shelves, books on navigation and seamanship. Evidently David took his cruising seriously. No sign of Joseph's interests; he seemed to have withdrawn almost completely into his own room. Over the years he had built up a life for himself, following well-trodden paths, asking little except to be left alone. Then David had wanted to come into the firm. Well, that was reasonable, no doubt he was entitled to his share and he had modern ideas. Together they would prosper and Joseph must have thought that he would be relieved of some of the drudgery and responsibility.

But it hadn't worked out like that; in less than three years David had destroyed the basis of his security and contentment and involved him in activities which threatened bankruptcy and worse. Not surprising if Joseph saw no point in carrying on; the man with his paperweights could have been the last straw. Not surprising then if Joseph had committed suicide. But if he had, why had the gun been removed? Why had fingerprints been wiped off in the office behind the shop? And where was David?

He crossed the passage to Joseph's room and pushed open the door. The room looked undisturbed. Joseph could have walked in, taken his seat at the desk and carried on where he had left off. Wycliffe felt pleased with his men; there was scarcely a sign of the meticulous examination to which the room had been subjected. A little square of carpet missing – that was all.

Out of curiosity he looked through Joseph's bookshelves for Coleridge's book on Chippendale – the book Bunny Lane said he had handed to David during his stroll on Saturday evening. There it was. He took down the book and opened it; the fly-leaf was inscribed in an old-fashioned copy-book hand, 'Michael Lane'. At first this seemed to be confirmation of Lane's story but then it struck him as odd that a book, casually handed in three-quarters of an hour after Joseph's death, should find its way into his shelves. Was it likely that David would have taken the book upstairs to the dead man's room and put it in the shelves? It was odd. Very odd indeed.

He went down the spiral staircase which seemed to vibrate even more noisily in the deserted building, and into the office. Here too everything looked much the same as when he had first seen it. He checked the safe door to make sure that it was locked; they had found the keys in Joseph's pocket. Then the telephone made him jump.

He picked it up and gave the number.

A man's voice said, 'Is that Mr Clement?'

He explained that Mr Clement was not available but offered to take a message.

'Ah! That will do. I've been trying to get hold of him since yesterday but there's been no reply. My name is Vincent – James Vincent of Porton House, Manningtree, Essex. I saw his advertisement in yesterday's issue of *Power Boat* and I'm interested in making an offer for *Manna*. I shall be free to come down at the weekend. If he could ring me . . . '

So David had planned to sell *Manna*; that made sense. It would have been too tricky to take her with him into his new life and he was not the sort to leave several thousand pounds' worth of boat as a memento to St Juliot. It meant that he was winding up his affairs preparatory to bowing out; it also meant that he hadn't intended to go when he did.

Wycliffe made his way through the shop, dodging the pieces of furniture, to the front door where several envelopes lay on the mat below the letter-box. He picked them up and sorted them on the nearest table. Bills and circulars. Nothing there.

He let himself out by the side-door and walked down the street to the newsagent on the corner where he bought a copy of *Power Boat*. He was among the first of Annie's lunch-time customers.

'Fricassee of chicken – how will that suit you?'

'Very well.'

'Shall I bring you a lager?'

Hesitation. 'No, I'll have a half-bottle of white Bordeaux.'

'Celebrating?'

'More like getting into training.'

While he waited he turned the pages of *Power Boat* and found Clement's advertisement: 'Motor cruiser, *Manna*. 4 berth OAL 30ft . . . '

He was back at the office by two o'clock feeling sleepy due to the wine. Kersey had left word for him to ring the Bournemouth police.

'It's extension 57, sir.'

'Get him for me, will you?'

The office seemed stuffy. Air conditioning! As if a man needed to be cultured like plants in a greenhouse! He often recalled with nostalgia his early days in the west country, before this present glass-and-concrete horror was built. He had his office in a Queen Anne building. It had an ornamental plaster ceiling, a wainscot and a marble fireplace which burned coal. When you felt cold or disgruntled you threw on another lump and imagined that you were burning your troubles. Most changes in the past twenty years had been, in his opinion, for the worse. Now they wanted to shut him up in a padded cell for the rest of his working life.

'Kersey?'

'Ah, thanks for ringing back, sir. I've got some news. There's no doubt that Clement and Page are the same – the caretaker of the flats and two or three of the tenants identified Page when I showed them Clement's photograph. The story is that he's a traveller for some firm dealing in cheap jewellery and fancy goods. He spends a few days a month in the flat, he has next to no mail and few visitors. Several times a girl has stayed there for a night or two, sometimes with Page, sometimes alone. One of the tenants and the caretaker identified Molly Stokes.

'Next, by visiting the local banks and being a bit devious I found that Page kept an account at the London and Counties in Gervis Place. My reception there was a bit frosty but when I'd explained that Page was an impostor the manager was more co-operative. Page opened his account two-and-a-half years ago on a reference from a firm of jewellers. The account has been fairly active but never overdrawn. Page has been buying securities in a straight forward way and depositing them with his bank. That was as far as I could get.'

It was far enough and the picture held no surprises but the crucial question remained. What had happened to Clement/Page?

That afternoon Wycliffe met reporters in the briefing room at headquarters. The case had attracted little attention at first, now it was beginning to interest the national press, radio and TV. For some reason antique dealers and the sea, like children and animals, are always newsworthy. With a bonus link to the London art robberies the combination was irresistable. He put his cards on the table in the hope that publicity might help rather than hinder.

'Do you think Clement came ashore in the dinghy, Mr Wycliffe?'

'I wish I knew.'

'Are you continuing to look for him in this area?'

'In this area and elsewhere; we are anxious to find both the boat and the man.'

'If Clement is found will he be arrested?'

'If Mr Clement is found he will be asked to help with our enquiries.'

'There are rumours that he took a large sum of money with him.'

'I know nothing about that.'

'Why was his car driven into the quarry?'

'Presumably it was intended to hide the car for as long as possible to delay an investigation.'

'Are you satisfied that Waddington was not concerned in Joseph Clement's death?'

'We don't expect to bring any charge against Waddington.'

'But what about the art robberies?'

'They are not our concern. Waddington is now in the custody of the Metropolitan police.'

'Isn't it a boost for West Country police in general and for you in particular that these robberies should have been solved down here after two years of work by Scotland Yard?'

'It would be quite wrong to think in those terms; a great many investigations involve co-operation between forces and success or failure is a joint responsibility. Often, as in this case, it is largely a matter of luck.'

Afterwards he had to say much the same thing to the TV cameras outside.

Back in his office he grumbled about a wasted afternoon but he was not very clear about what else he would have done. It was five o'clock.

'I'm going home.'

'But—'

'No buts, Diane! I'll see you in the morning.'

They were surprised to see him so early and he was surprised by the elegant and sophisticated young woman his daughter had become. Her new job and her new boss had changed her. He felt absurdly shy until she put her arms round his neck and kissed him in the old way.

'I'm afraid I have to go out again later.'

'How much later?'

He muttered, shamefaced, 'Half-past seven to eight.'

'Then we must eat early.' Helen's response was a good deal milder than he had feared.

While they were eating he said, 'The Oldroyds want us to come to their place on Wednesday.'

'But we were there less than three weeks ago and we haven't had them back.'

'I know, but I think we'd better go.'

'Is there something on?'

'It's confidential at the moment but Bellings is going and Oldroyd wants me to apply.'

Ruth said, 'But that's marvellous! With Mr Oldroyd's backing there wouldn't be much doubt, would there?'

'Probably not, if I applied.'

'If? Surely . . .'

Helen came to his rescue. 'It's not as simple as that; the work is quite different and your father may not feel that he wants to make a change.'

'But won't it have a big effect on your salary and on your pension? In these days it's income you have to think of – not capital . . .'

Wycliffe was constantly surprised by his children. At one moment you were feeding them on purée and rusks, at the next they are telling you how to plan for your old age.

'Don't you think your brother ought to be in on this?'

Ruth looked at him, her face blank. 'David?'

'If we are going to make the decision in family committee.'

It took a moment to sink in then she blushed and laughed at the same time.

'I'm sorry. Richard is always telling me that I'm too ready to offer advice.'

'Richard?'

'Richard Locksley, my boss.'

He left the house at a little before eight and drove to Bear Street to park in front of the old custom-house. This was part of his ritual for the case. It was a dry night and the air was still. He walked the short distance to St John's Court and knocked on the door of Lane's cottage. Footsteps in the stone passage, a key turned and the door opened. Lane stood, his stocky figure silhouetted against the light from the open door of the living-room.

'Mr Wycliffe! I wasn't expecting you. You'd better come in . . . ' Not a gushing welcome. Lane helped the superintendent off with his coat and hung it on one of several pegs in the passage. The major's duffle coat was there and two or three cloth caps.

'I've got company tonight, but you know Major Parkyn.'

Wycliffe made no bones about it. 'Yes, being a Thursday, I guessed that I might find you together.'

It was as he had imagined it. Parkyn was relaxed in one of the three armchairs, his long legs stretched out to the fire; comfort beyond anything Garrison Drive could offer. He was in the act of lighting his pipe. Lane's pipe smouldered in a large ashtray placed on a low stool between the two chairs.

Lane pulled forward the third chair. 'Sit there, Mr Wycliffe. I believe you are a pipe smoker so carry on if you want to.'

The major acknowledged him with a nod which, if not cordial, was not disagreeable either. The room was over-warm but cosy. Lane drew a curtain across the door to exclude possible draughts. The box of dominoes was already in place on the square kitchen table. Wycliffe couldn't help thinking, 'If I were Joseph Clement . . . ' He filled his pipe, taking plenty of time as it was proper to do. The alarm clock on the mantelpiece showed half-past eight. It had a shiny metal case which gave the tick a metallic echo, clink-clink, clink-clink . . .

Bunny Lane sat down and reached for his pipe.

Wycliffe said, 'I came for information and advice.' He turned to Lane. 'You told me that you went for a stroll at some time before ten on Saturday night and that you dropped in a book which you had promised to lend Joseph.'

'That's true.' Lane puffed away at his pipe.

'You saw a light at the back of the shop, tapped on the glass door, and David came out – is that right?'

'That is so.'

'Did you go into the shop?'

'No, I told you; I handed in the book and left.'

So as not to disturb the tempo of the proceedings he allowed a long pause. 'I am asking you this because a new witness has told us two things; first, that she heard what was probably the shot which killed Joseph at a little after nine; second, that she saw a stocky, oldish man wearing a cloth cap, come up the street from the direction of the harbour at a little before ten. This man appeared to tap on the shop door which was opened to him and he went in.'

Lane smiled, briefly exposing his teeth and his hare-lip. 'She must have seen me but she's got it a bit wrong.'

'I see. But you understand how important it is. David must have answered the door to you less than an hour after the shot.'

Lane nodded. 'It looks that way if your witness is reliable but it's difficult to believe.'

Lane was being either completely honest or he was clever enough not to protest too much.

'Just one more question, do you have a car?'

Lane looked surprised. 'Not a car; I have a little van which I use to deliver things I've made or worked on.'

Parkyn shifted heavily in his chair, causing the springs to creak. Lane glanced at the clock. He said, 'About this time, Mr Wycliffe, we usually have a drink. If you would like to join us . . .'

'I wouldn't say no to a glass of your wine.'

Lane got up and went through to the back kitchen. Parkyn continued to smoke, staring into the fire which had a glowing orange-red centre. The clock ticked a couple of minutes away then Lane came back with a tin tray on which he had a bottle of wine, a bottle of whisky, three glasses polished so that the light glistened on them, and an earthenware pitcher of water. He removed the ashtray and put the tray on the stool.

'Help yourself, Mr Wycliffe. Whisky if you prefer it.'

'No thanks, I'll stick to wine.'

Parkyn put his pipe in his pocket, leaned forward and poured himself a generous whisky to which he added a spoonful of water.

'Your very good health!' He took a gulp of the spirit and sighed deeply.

'Cheers!' Wycliffe sipped his wine. 'I believe that at one time you used to do some sailing round this coast, Major?'

The grey, slightly bulging eyes regarded him with an expressionless stare which might have intimidated the less hardened, and it was some time before he answered, 'I had a boat for a while when I first retired.'

'A sail or power boat?'

'Sail with auxiliary diesel.'

'So you know the coast pretty well.'

Parkyn took another gulp of whisky and wiped his lips before replying, 'I don't recall getting lost.'

'Are you a boating man, Mr Lane?'

Lane got up and placed fresh lumps of coal on the fire, arranging them strategically. 'Not me; I like dry land under my feet.'

Wycliffe said, 'I expect you know that David Clement seems to have cleared off in his motor cruiser and that her dinghy was found adrift off Hucket's Cove on Sunday morning, rowlocks in place, planks stove in.'

He waited for some acknowledgement but hardly

expected to get one. However, after the mandatory interval, Parkyn said, 'Hucket's is in Porthellin Bay; what was he doing in there?'

'Our first idea was that he had lost his dinghy.'

'Anything is possible with the fools who take to the water these days.' The major emptied his glass and leaned forward to replenish it; this time he added no water.

'The boatmen at St Juliot say that he was very competent.'

'Ah!'

'I would be obliged by your opinion. It seems to me possible that Clement rowed ashore at Hucket's. You see, *Manna* had only enough fuel for forty miles yet, despite the fact that we have alerted every port up and down the channel, there has been no news of her.'

Parkyn brought out his pipe again, knocked it out on the fender and turned to Wycliffe. 'Are you suggesting that he left her adrift and that she's bobbing about out there in the channel?'

'No, I'm suggesting that he scuttled her.'

Parkyn raised his great shoulders in a slow shrug indicating that there was no more to be said.

'And I'm considering the best way of finding her.'

Parkyn was filling his pipe from an old oil-skin pouch, his large, freckled hands seemed capable of remarkable precision of movement, there was nothing clumsy about his broad, square-tipped fingers. At Wycliffe's remark he stopped what he was doing and once more stared at the superintendent, then he laughed. 'I wish you joy, Mr Wycliffe! There's a hell of a lot of water within rowing distance of Hucket's.'

Lane sipped his wine and smoked his pipe which made little bubbling sounds but he said nothing.

'I understand that there was quite a strong breeze from the south-east on Saturday night and in these circumstances, with an ebbing tide, they tell me that there wouldn't be much chance for a small dinghy unless she was sheltered by the crook of Laira.'

Parkyn, having filled his pipe, proceeded to light it. Only when he had finished and it was drawing nicely did he make any comment. 'I gather you've taken professional advice.'

'From Sam Foster the harbour master.'

'I see.'

'Would you agree with his assessment?'

'I wouldn't disagree; I don't know enough about it.'

'It seems that when one takes into account the shallow areas and the nature of the bottom there is a relatively small area in which *Manna* could have been scuttled without the possibility of her showing up again on the next ebb.'

Parkyn nodded. 'That's very interesting, but why would Clement put to sea at St Juliot only to scuttle his boat and go ashore in Porthellin Bay?'

'Perhaps on the principle that it's safest to hide near home?'

Parkyn shook his head. 'It doesn't seem very likely to me.'

The fresh coals took fire in little spurts of blue and yellow flame and the clock sustained its monotonous metallic tick. It was twenty minutes past nine. Parkyn was becoming restless again, shifting his position so that the springs of the old chair constantly protested. In the end, almost shamefaced, he said, 'I don't suppose you play dominoes, Mr Wycliffe?'

'I did at one time but it's a long time ago.'

'But you do know the rules?'

'More or less.'

Parkyn's face brightened. 'It will soon come back.' He took another great gulp of spirit. 'I expect Mr Wycliffe could do with topping-up, Bunny.'

They played in silence, sitting on the bent-wood chairs at the big square table which was covered with oil-cloth. Two or three times Bunny replenished their glasses and once he got up to put fresh coal on the fire. When the little shiny clock showed twenty minutes to twelve the major stood up. 'I must be going; I've already overstayed my time. Thank you for a pleasant evening.' The only effect of all that he had drunk was to make him rather slower in his movements, rather more precise in his speech.

Wycliffe said, 'I'll come part of the way with you, Major.'

Was he consciously doing what he supposed Joseph would have done?

Bunny saw them to the door. Outside it was a quiet clear night; so quiet that they could have been in the country. Their footsteps echoed through the deserted square and as they turned down into Bear Street they caught the fresh, salty tang of the sea.

'A pleasant evening, Wycliffe.' Wycliffe noted that he had been received into the major's orbit and was none too pleased though he realized that he had only himself to blame. Again, as they separated, it was 'Good-night to you, Wycliffe. Perhaps we shall be able to do that again.'

'Good-night, Major.'

CHAPTER SEVEN

A myth with a long pedigree would have us believe that scientific research consists in being open-minded and doing experiments until some inescapable conclusion is forced on the experimenter by the logic of his results. Of course, nobody ever has worked like that or ever could. A researcher starts with a notional conclusion (hunch) and devises experiments to find out whether it will stand up. A detective works in the same way and for the detective, as for the scientist, his work is as good as his hunches. But policemen and scientists and other people too, prefer to believe that their actions are guided by the pure light of impeccable logic.

Wycliffe was no exception, he was ashamed of his hunches and he had to wrestle with his conscience over them especially when, as now, playing a hunch was likely to cost the taxpayer money. It troubled him over his toast and marmalade.

'I shouldn't worry about it; after all, the main thing is to do what you are happiest doing.' Ruth, making a long arm for the marmalade.

He looked at her, puzzled. 'What on earth are you talking about?'

Helen laughed. 'You see! I wouldn't mind betting that it hasn't entered his head since we were talking about it last night.'

Which wasn't entirely true. In the lazy interval between sleeps at about four in the morning, he had tried to think himself behind the padded door without much success.

He was in his office by twenty minutes past eight, beating Kersey by a short head.

'I came back last night, sir. What's on the menu?'

'Trawling in Porthellin Bay. I'm going to have an area trawled for *Manna*.'

Kersey's bushy eyebrows went up. 'Something new?'

'No. It's just that the longer we go without news of either *Manna* or Clement, the more convinced I am that he didn't leave the antique shop of his own accord. He wasn't the sort to walk out and leave a small fortune behind. I'm beginning to wonder if he left the place alive.'

Kersey looked solemn. 'You think he might be down there with his boat?'

'It's a possibility.'

'If so we shall be all the more interested in the guy who went ashore.'

'Exactly. And this is what I want you to do: inquiries at Porthellin and at any houses along the coast. It's my guess that our man landed at Hucket's where he stood little chance of being seen but he might have had the nerve to come ashore at the slip-way or even the jetty. After all it must have been dark or only just beginning to get light. You may come across an insomniac or it's possible that there were boats out long-lining; I gather they still do it in a small way.'

When Kersey had gone Wycliffe telephoned Foster. 'I've decided to go ahead with the search and I'm wondering whether you can advise me about the hire of a suitable boat and crew?'

Foster was obviously pleased. 'I'll set it up for you if you like. I must confess I shall get a bit of a kick out of it. Of course I shall have to do it through Ron Bryce at Porthellin but that's no problem.'

'Good! That would certainly be a weight off my mind.'

'When do you want to start?'

'Yesterday.'

Foster chuckled. 'I'll see what I can do; I suppose you want it kept as quiet as possible?'

'On the contrary, the more publicity the better.'

So that was that.

He lunched at Annie's and in the afternoon there was Joseph's funeral.

It was a surprise to see the little chapel full and it was not until the mourners gathered round the grave that he was able to sort them out. Molly Stokes was there and she seemed to share the role of chief mourner with Bunny Lane; an incongruous pair. Molly wore a dark green winter coat and carried an umbrella. Wycliffe was surprised to see how pale she was and once when their eyes met across the open grave he fancied that she looked at him less as a threat than as someone to turn to.

Head and shoulders above the rest, in a heavy service-mackintosh which had seen better days, the major looked neither to the right nor the left. His bulging eyes seemed to be focused on the far distance. Annie Blazek was there and Friend, the lawyer. Friend's eyes were moist and he was flushed; from time to time he turned aside to blow his nose in a grubby handkerchief. A couple of journalists and a photographer hovered on the fringe and the rest were almost certainly tradespeople from the street, members of the Bear Street Traders' Association, a significant lobby in city affairs.

When the service was over Wycliffe drove straight back to his office. A fallow day. At five o'clock he picked up the telephone and asked for his home number.

'Ruth? . . . How would you and your mother like to eat out tonight?'

There was a brief consultation followed by agreement.

'I'll book a table.'

He telephoned the restaurant in Bear Street and booked a table for three at eight-thirty.

At nine o'clock the Wycliffe's were starting their main course: *Porc dijonnaise*. The restaurant was full and Annie had an assistant, a girl Wycliffe had not seen before. There was a hum of conversation, a rattle of knives and forks, and the windows were steamed over. Wycliffe looked surreptitiously at his watch and as he did so he heard a sound like a firework going off, muffled and distant. He glanced round the room; no-one else seemed to have noticed.

Kersey had fired the general's revolver in Joseph Clement's room and Marilyn Ford was co-operating to the extent that she had agreed to remain in her room though she had not been told for what purpose. By chance the conditions were almost identical with what they had been on the night Joseph died; it had rained for most of the day and Bear Street was deserted.

On Saturday morning it was a relief to look out of the window and see the estuary sparkling under a watery sun; it made him realize how much he was counting on the operation in Porthellin Bay.

'Six days shalt thou labour and do all thy work . . . ' For most of us the divine ordinance has been cut to five and though he commonly worked six and sometimes seven, Wycliffe enjoyed a greater sense of freedom at weekends and felt more at liberty to follow his nose. He would not let his anxiety about the trawling get the better of him and he took a leisurely breakfast so that when Ruth came down in her dressing gown at nine o'clock he was still at the table.

'Not going in today?'

'Later.'

'That was a good meal last night, dad. Is she a friend of yours?'

'The way things are, you might say that we are colleagues.'

At half-past nine he drove to Bear Street, walked to

Godolphin Street and rang the bell of Molly Stokes's flat.

She opened the door wearing an old pair of slacks, a cotton top and with her hair caught back by a piece of ribbon; she had no make-up on.

'Have you heard something?'

He followed her into the living-room where the remains of her breakfast were still on the table.

'I wanted to tell you that I was in the antique shop yesterday when a man telephoned to say that he'd seen David's advertisement in *Power Boat* and wanted to make a bid for *Manna*.'

'So?'

'Isn't it obvious that David was planning to get out but that he went before he intended?'

She was tense, very near to tears but she was not the crying sort and her emotion exploded in anger. 'All right! All bloody right! He's gone, but where? You're the policeman, so find him!' Driven to some sort of activity, she started to clear the breakfast things away, carrying them through to her little kitchen.

He watched her for a moment then he said, 'I'm having part of Porthellin Bay trawled, starting this morning.'

She stopped in her tracks. 'Trawled. What for?'

'For *Manna*.'

She put the flat of her hand to her forehead in a helpless gesture. 'Oh, God!'

'Don't think I know anything which you don't. I've no idea what they will find, if anything. You and I are asking the same questions.'

She looked as though she wanted to believe him and he added, 'The point is, the longer we go on with no news the less likely it seems that David left of his own accord.'

She took out a cigarette with a trembling hand, and lit it. 'That's where I'd got when I came back from Bournemouth. But who would force him to leave and why?' She stood with one hand resting on the back of his chair, smoking nervously. 'His whole future depended on the Bournemouth set-up; even if he wanted to ditch me, he couldn't afford to let that go.' After a pause she said, 'It doesn't look too good, does it?'

Wycliffe stood up. 'Try not to worry too much. I'll let you know as soon as I have anything fresh to tell you.'

She came with him to the door, reluctant to let him go.

As he turned the corner into Bear Street he saw the major coming out of the betting shop and he began to feel, in some strange way, that things were coming right. He was not sitting at a desk reading reports about people, he was out, meeting them. He waited and watched Parkyn trundle down the street to his next port of call, the mini-market.

A man's barber, his doctor, his priest, his children, his mistress and his wife have all been considered by different authorities as best placed to form a true estimate of his character. Nobody, it seems, has suggested his bookmaker – yet, for a betting man, the bookie is as likely to get it right as any of the others.

Wycliffe crossed the street to the betting office.

'Mr Lacey, please.'

The clerk recognized him and raised the counter flap. Wycliffe passed through a room where two more clerks were talking on telephones and knocked on a glass-panelled door.

Lacey looked more like a trendy parson than a bookie in his pepper-and-salt suiting, his quiet tie and discreetly striped shirt.

'Trouble, Mr Wycliffe?'

'Not for you. I want to pick your brains about Major Parkyn.'

Lacey took off his gold-rims and laid them in the middle of a huge form on which he had been working. 'Professional ethics, Mr Wycliffe.'

147

'I know all about that but I'd still like your opinion of Parkyn.'

'As a man or as a punter?'

'Doesn't it come to the same thing?'

Lacey grinned. 'You could be right. Anyway, it's a tall order; all I can say is that he isn't what he seems. I mean, if I didn't know him I'd say he was the sort who if he bet at all would put his money each-way on the favourite with an occasional flutter on a double.'

'But it's not like that?'

'No way! He'll go for two or three weeks, betting sensibly, even cleverly, until he's got a fair sum then, when his pension comes or whatever, he'll come in here and put the lot on some crazy accumulator which is sudden death – I know it and he knows it. In the early days, once or twice, I gave him a friendly warning but all I got for thanks was that cold, fishy look which makes you wonder if you've left your flies undone or something.' Lacey looked at Wycliffe and spoke with deliberation. 'I'm quite sure that these crazy gambles are the only ones which give him a kick – the rest are build up.'

'And when he loses?'

'No effect.' Lacey picked up his glasses. 'No apparent effect, anyway.'

'Has he ever come up.'

'Once in the five or six years he's been with me. I can't remember the amount but it was several thousand and he'd lost it again in weeks rather than months.'

'Was he thrilled at winning?'

'Not so's you'd notice. Underneath, he's some sort of wild man, Mr Wycliffe. I can't explain it but it seems to me he's one of those chaps who's always got to be on a tightrope.'

Wycliffe did not go back to his car, instead he walked along the street and up Dog's Leg Lane to Garrison Drive. The sun was shining through a thin mist making the air luminescent, and somewhere someone was

148

mowing grass. The Parkyn house stood out like a sore thumb among its pampered neighbours but he had not come to visit the Parkyns. He walked the length of Garrison Drive which ended in a wooden fence with a stile and a notice which read, 'Footpath only to Porthellin.' From the top of the stile he could see the whole of the bay with the village in the far corner. Between the village and the crook of Laira the little shingle beach which was Hucket's Cove stood out white against the sombre cliffs. He could just make out a small boat which seemed to be cruising parallel with the shore. It was ten minutes past eleven.

He followed the footpath which soon joined the road and the road pursued a devious course round the margins of the bay to the village. The walk took him about forty-five minutes and must have been close on three miles. To Hucket's Cove would be another mile-and-a-half. He walked through the almost deserted village to the quay. There was little sign of activity, just a knot of men on the eastern jetty looking out to sea; one of them was Foster, the others were villagers.

'Well, we've made a start, Mr Wycliffe,' Foster said. 'We're using Bert Cundy's *Blue Boy*, she's more manoeuvrable than the bigger boats. Ron Bryce is out there with Bert.'

The blue launch looked insignificant in the great expanse of water and the crooked headland seemed far away. Wycliffe was shaken, the operation which had seemed reasonable on the chart now looked absurd. A needle in a haystack!

'You see those four dan buoys, Mr Wycliffe? They mark the four corners of our pitch, so to speak.'

After a moment of looking Wycliffe could see four little flags sticking up out of the water.

'It's like ploughing a field, but when you're ploughing the hedges stay still unless you've had a few. Here they don't; although each of the dan buoys is anchored with

149

a grapnel on the bottom and won't shift, the buoys themselves move with the tide and wind. We've got to allow for that.'

'Yes, I see.'

'Good! Now look at the two nearer buoys. Can you see a line of floats between them?'

'Yes.'

'Well there's a similar line of floats between the two outer buoys which you probably can't see from here. The floats are ten yards apart and they help Bert to keep a line. On this game you can't look back and see the furrow.'

Wycliffe did not want to ask the question but he felt driven to it. 'How long do you think it will take?'

Foster pursed his lips and frowned. 'Well, I reckon he's got to do the length of the course at least a hundred and twenty times, which mean's he's got to cover forty miles. Towing the trawl he's not making more than three knots so that makes thirteen hours to cover the ground and that's not allowing for a certain amount of double-tracking which is bound to happen.' Foster lifted his uniform cap and smoothed his bald head. 'He got started about eight so he's unlikely to finish today unless he finds something. You can't work in the dark on this game and he'll have to have a break now and then.'

Wycliffe watched the launch traverse a length, turn, and come back down the course. It was exceedingly boring. He had to admit that he had arrived with a certain excitement, now he felt let down.

'What about divers, Mr Wycliffe?'

'Divers?'

'You're going to need 'em if we strike something.'

'But not today?'

'No, if we're lucky enough to pick her up today we shall put out a marker buoy but then you would need them tomorrow. I think we should contact the navy because tomorrow's Sunday and it might not be easy unless we give them notice. They'll insist on using their own boats. You know what they are; any boat that doesn't carry the white ensign must have a hole in her bottom and they don't like getting their feet wet.'

Wycliffe did not answer at once; he had to admit to himself that he had lost confidence in the whole operation.

'I'll get on to them if you like, Mr Wycliffe. We speak the same lingo.'

'I'd be glad if you would.' Wycliffe felt ashamed of himself.

Foster looked at him with a faint smile. 'We'll find her if she's there. There's no point in you hanging about though. It's sure to be a long job.'

Wycliffe returned home and tried to put *Manna* out of his mind. It was a glorious April day and Helen and Ruth were working in the garden. After lunch Foster telephoned to say that the navy had agreed 'In principle' to provide divers once the boat had been located but they wanted Wycliffe to attend at the Admiral Superintendent's office to deal with documentation.

Two hours of exquisitely polite Arab-tea-party chit-chat confirmed him in his total ignorance of salvage law and worried him the more about the documents he had to sign. But at the finish, the officer, a lieutenant-commander, said, 'Not to worry old chap. On these salvage larks you can't go wrong; either you get your money back with interest from the owner or you flog the thing and make a bomb. I've often thought of taking it up as a business when they put me out to grass.'

At six o'clock he drove to Porthellin, feeling distinctly edgy. The village lay serene in the evening sun. *Blue Boy*, Bert Cundy's launch, was moored in the basin, riding high with the tide which was only an hour past the flood. Out in the bay, three of the dan buoys and the floats had gone and a single buoy remained as a marker, hopefully, indicating the position of *Manna*.

He found Bert Cundy and Ron Bryce in the bar.

'We got her in less than seven hours, Mr Wycliffe,' Bryce said.

'You think it's the *Manna*?'

'If it isn't it's something very like her.'

'We tried 'er from all ways,' Bert said. 'O' course it was coming up to 'igh water so we couldn't see nothing.'

'What are you drinking?'

'Pints will do us, Mr Wycliffe.'

The atmosphere in the pub was intimate and friendly; all the regulars seemed to take satisfaction in a job well done. 'When you come to the sea, Mr Wycliffe, there's nobody on these coasts to touch a Porthellin man.'

'What happens now?'

Ron Bryce ran his hand through his curly black thatch. 'That depends on the navy but if they'll only get their fingers out they could lift her tomorrow morning. It's low water at half-eleven. If they go down and get their hawsers attached by then, that's all we shall want 'em for. We then stand by until about a quarter to six in the evening for high water and tow her into the basin.'

Wycliffe had seen this sort of thing done once before * 'Then we shall have to wait for the tide to go down again and leave her high and dry. Is that it?'

'In a nutshell, Mr Wycliffe. You'd be able to go aboard her sometime before midnight tomorrow night. After that, it depends.'

'What depends?'

Bryce sank the best part of half-a-pint in one swallow. 'Well, if she was scuttled by opening her sea-cock all we got to do is shut it and she'll rise like a bird on the next tide, but if she's got any planks stove in then they'll have to be botched up before she'll ride.'

It all sounded simple and reassuring.

He arrived home again just before nine. There was a

---

* *Wycliffe and the Pea-Green Boat.*

message from Foster to say that the navy would be on the job in the morning – weather permitting. He listened to the forecast. 'Continuing fine at first tomorrow, with long sunny periods, but rain will reach the south-west later in the day with strengthening winds.'

Was it too much to ask that for once a poor, struggling policeman might be favourably noticed by Providence?

CHAPTER EIGHT

Sunday morning, exactly a week since he had found the gun on the beach at St Juliot, and another Oh-to-be-in-England day, but no leisurely stroll along the shore to collect his newspaper.

'Will you be home for lunch?'

'I expect so but I shall have to go out again.'

He would probably spend the day waiting around. On the assumption that all would go well he had arranged for Kersey and three men to be available with an emergency vehicle and floodlamps for work after dark.

He drove to Porthellin and arrived there shortly after eight to find the navy already in possession. Two un-naval looking craft, like grey tubs, were anchored near the remaining dan-buoy and several men were moving about in them. One of the boats carried a number of white cylinders which Wycliffe supposed to be the floats which (fingers crossed) would, with the help of the tide, eventually lift *Manna* clear of the bottom.

Ron Bryce and Bert Cundy were on the quay, grumbling. 'A toffee-nosed sub-lieut as good as told us to keep out of the way.'

Foster arrived and joined the group. He glanced at his watch. 'Eight forty-five; I don't think they'll start diving until half-past nine at the earliest, that would give them more than two hours to low water and they'd be working in under five fathom.'

In fact, it was a little after nine-thirty when the first wet-suited diver went over the side. He was down for a minute or two and when he came up two others went down to surface again after a couple of minutes.

Ron Bryce said, 'You'd think the bastards would signal or something.'

As though Bryce had been overheard, one of the divers raised his hand in the thumbs-up sign.

Wycliffe breathed a sigh of relief.

There was a lull, then the divers went down again and each appeared to be carrying a line. The church clock chimed and struck ten. The watchers on the quay were joined by others, including a contingent of children. The sun was shining and the bay sparkled under an almost cloudless sky.

'The weather looks good.'

Bert Cundy grimaced and squinted at the sky. 'All right for a few hours but there's rain and wind on the way.'

'That's what they said in the weather forecast.'

'Then they'm right for once.'

One of the navy vessels had shifted her position and eight of the floats were now bobbing about in the water between the two boats. The church bell tolled for the morning service. There had been several more dives and now the divers were swimming about on the surface, manoeuvring the floats.

The ebb was running out now and in the basin boats were lying over on their beam ends or resting on their legs. The water was running away in rivulets and streams leaving the muddy, weedy bottom exposed. Bert Cundy spat down into the mud.

'It's going to be a bit tight, Mr Wycliffe. I was out there this morning on top of the tide – at 'alf past five. I took a few soundings with a lead line and I reckon she was lying in six fathom – that's thirty-six feet of water. We'll get about a nineteen or twenty foot tide, so, when they lift 'er she'll still be sixteen or seventeen feet down – do you follow me?'

'Yes. You mean that when the tide has lifted her she'll still be under sixteen or seventeen feet of water.'

'Exactly. And we shall 'ave about eighteen foot of water in the basin so there's going to be little enough to spare but I reckon we'll manage.'

Foster said, 'Look! They're taking up the slack on the hawsers.'

Wycliffe could see the floats coming into line, two lines of four. He glanced at his watch, it was eleven-thirty – eight minutes to low water.

'You got to 'and it to 'em; they're doing a fair job,' Cundy conceded.

Foster said, 'There's nothing we can do now except keep an eye on her until high water this evening. No point in you hanging about, Mr Wycliffe.'

He was not unwilling to escape. He drove to Bear Street, up Dog's Leg Lane and out to Garrison Drive. It was a week to the hour since he had first made acquaintance with the major. He rang the door-bell and in a little while the door was opened by the major himself.

'Ah! Wycliffe. You come most carefully upon your hour.' He stood aside to let Wycliffe through. 'Second door on your right.'

It was the little room in which they had talked the previous Monday evening. Although it was warm outside the paraffin heater was on and the room seemed oppressively stuffy. He waved to a chair and sat down himself. His pipe and a box of matches rested on the arm of his chair and there was a glass of whisky on the floor at his feet.

'Smoke if you want to . . . Will you have a drink?'

'Not just now, thanks.'

How much time did Parkyn spend in this bare little room, curled up like a dog in its kennel?

'Have you a telephone in the house?'

'Telephone? No, I've no use for the thing.'

'How about Lane?'

Parkyn turned slowly in his chair to look at Wycliffe before saying, 'He's got a telephone. I suppose he needs it for his business; I don't have any business.'

'We think we have located Clement's boat.'

'Ah!'

'On the bottom, off Hucket's Cove.'

'So you were right.'

'Someone must have scuttled the launch, rowed ashore in the dinghy and walked from the cove, probably before daylight on Sunday morning, but there's quite a chance he might have been seen.'

Parkyn, in the middle of lighting his pipe, gave him a sideways glance. 'You think so? Are you going to get her up – the launch, I mean?'

'Navy divers were out there this morning; they've attached floats and we are hoping that she will lift with tonight's tide and that we shall be able to tow her into the basin.'

Surely Parkyn must have seen something of the activity in the bay?

'She can't be very deep if you can lift her with the tide alone.'

'No, she's lying in about six fathoms at high water.'

'You are fortunate.'

There was a prolonged silence during which Parkyn smoked contentedly and there was no atmosphere of tension. When Wycliffe spoke again it was in the manner he might have adopted in discussing a troublesome case with a colleague.

'It's a complicated story and there are too many gaps but I'm hoping that we shall be able to close some of them when we've raised *Manna*. There's no doubt that David Clement was a crook, involved with a gang of London thieves, and that he fenced their stolen property through the firm. One of his associates called by appointment on Saturday evening at eight o'clock.

David was out and Joseph admitted the visitor but David arrived shortly afterwards and Joseph left them to their business in the office behind the shop.'

The feeling of the little room was not the same as in Bunny Lane's kitchen. This was the refuge of a solitary man. Parkyn stooped for his glass, 'Sure you won't join me?'

'Not just now.'

Parkyn drank some whisky and sighed.

'The visitor left at about eight-forty and at nine o'clock David was in the *Seven Stars*. At about this time a neighbour heard a bang which was probably the shot which killed Joseph. Less than an hour later the same neighbour saw a stocky, oldish man, wearing a peaked cap, go to the shop door. The witness says that the shop was in darkness but that someone came to the door and let him in.'

Wycliffe paused. 'I'm not boring you?'

'By no means.'

'At some time after one o'clock another neighbour was awakened by a car being driven down the back lane behind the shops. Between two and three in the morning, witnesses at St Juliot heard a car reversing off the jetty. On Sunday morning I found your father's revolver within a few feet of the jetty, lying on the shingle not far below high-water mark.'

Parkyn shifted heavily in his chair but said nothing.

'On Monday Joseph Clement's body was found in his room, according to the pathologist he had died some time on Saturday of a bullet wound in the head. The ballistics expert says that he was shot with your father's gun.' Wycliffe broke off and moved his chair back a little further from the heater. 'If it hadn't been for the absence of a weapon we should have treated the case as suicide and I am still inclined to think that is what it was. However, we found afterwards that *Manna* had been moved from her moorings, David Clement's car was

158

discovered in St Juliot's quarry, *Manna*'s dinghy turned up damaged and adrift off Hucket's Cove and now we have *Manna* herself sunk in the bay. With all this there has been no news of David Clement since he was seen by Bunny Lane on Saturday evening.'

In the silence which followed the only sound was Parkyn's deep, almost laboured breathing. In the end Parkyn said, 'It's a strange tale – difficult to see how it can all be made to hang together.'

'You have no suggestions to make?'

'Me? Good God, no! I'm not good at that sort of thing. Not my line at all.'

The two men looked at each other for some time and it would have been hard to say which had out-stared the other, but finally Wycliffe got to his feet.

'Are you going?'

'I won't keep you from your lunch and I must get home to mine.'

Parkyn followed him into the hall. Hetty was standing near the bottom of the stairs and she came forward. In a harsh voice she said, 'You are becoming a regular visitor, Mr Wycliffe.'

Wycliffe thought that she looked less composed than he had yet seen her; her grey hair was untidy and there was a wild look in her eyes. He said, 'I shall trouble you as little as possible, Miss Parkyn.'

Parkyn watched him down the slope to the road.

Back in his car he sat at the wheel for a while, indecisive, then he started the engine and drove home.

Helen and Ruth were drinking sherry in the kitchen, marking time before serving the meal. 'We had almost given you up.'

After lunch he sat in an armchair with a book and promptly fell asleep. When he woke he thought for a moment that he must have slept through the afternoon for the room was almost dark, then he saw the inky-black clouds which had crept up over the estuary and the white flecks on the sea whipped up by a freshening wind. As he watched the rain came sweeping in beating down on the water and on the shrubs in the garden which seemed to cower under its force. A quarter past four; in an hour or thereabouts they would begin towing *Manna* into the basin and he wondered how much the weather would interfere.

He found the two women in Helen's workroom, cutting out a dress. 'I have to go out. Expect me when you see me.'

He put on his heavy mackintosh and a fly-fisherman's hat of which he was secretly proud. He stowed a pair of wellingtons in the boot of the car. It rained heavily all the way to Porthellin and when he came in sight of the bay he was shocked by the grey turbulent waste which a few hours before had looked like a tourist poster. Bert Cundy's launch was in position, tossing up and down by the marker flag which rocked madly. He thought he could see two figures in the launch, one crouched over the tiller, the other by the decked-in fo'c'sle. Even in the shelter of the basin the swell was rocking the moored boats and slapping against the quay. He found Foster in the boatman's shelter with four or five other men.

'So Bert's out there already.'

'Oh, he's been out there since the tide began to make – him and Ron Bryce. You see, once she lifts, there's nothing to hold her but the kedge the navy put down and with this bit of sea we don't want accidents now. Bert's got a tow-line on her and in another half-hour or so he'll start bringing her in.'

At the entrance to the basin the swell was causing a rise and fall of two or three feet; it looked ominous but Foster was reassuring. 'There between the heads is the worst bit, there's a sort of bar, but if Bert plays his cards right the swell could help him. Caught right, it could lift *Manna* over.'

Wycliffe was given a cup of strong, scalding tea with scarcely any milk. The rain eased but the wind strengthened. One of the men said, 'I'll bet ol' Ron is as sick as a shag; 'e never could abide being moored up in a swell.'

They all laughed. Evidently the thought added spice to what was an enthralling spectator sport. At twenty minutes past five one of them said, 'He's drawing up on the kedge – there, she's free.'

'Won't be long now, Mr Wycliffe.'

It was a minute or two before he could detect any movement then he realized that the launch was creeping slowly nearer the shore. It was a slow business because the drag of the submerged *Manna* was considerable; however, the distance steadily diminished and at eighteen minutes to six the launch was between the heads, rising and falling with the swell and as she rose the men in her were level with their companions on the quay.

Foster said, 'He's towing on a short line so there's no risk of the tow fouling the heads.'

Cundy was at the tiller and Bryce, grey-faced, at the engine. Cundy was looking back over his shoulder, watching the floats and the progress of each swell. Suddenly he shouted, 'Now!' Bryce opened the throttle and the launch surged forward just as the swell lifted the white floats behind her. Foster said, 'Oopsa daisy!' and they saw the dim outline of the submerged *Manna*, like a giant fish, glide through into the basin. Foster heaved a great sigh of relief.

There was a certain amount of manoeuvring to get the cruiser into the most sheltered position, a mooring rope was thrown ashore, then Cundy dropped his tow and brought *Blue Boy* round to the steps. He came up, grinning, closely followed by Bryce who looked sorry for himself.

'She'll do nicely there, Mr Wycliffe. The twin-keels will keep 'er trim when the tide leaves 'er.'

Wycliffe realized that any particular show of appreciation would not be in order and he contented himself with a nod. 'Good!'

At ten-thirty that evening Wycliffe was back on the quay again, looking down at *Manna* whose super structure was already uncovered by the ebbing tide. The wind was still strong, there was white water in the bay and rain came in frequent and sudden squalls out of the darkness. But *Manna* lay snug in the shelter of the basin.

Sergeant Kersey arrived, closely followed by a police emergency vehicle carrying flood-lamps and a generator. The lights were switched on and directed down into the basin; their ghostly brilliance cast strange shadows and made the surrounding darkness seem even more impenetrable.

Kersey said, 'She's safe enough there, sir. There'll be another low at mid-day tomorrow and it will be a lot easier—'

Wycliffe cut him short. 'We are doing this tonight.'

The deck of the *Manna* was only a yard from one of the iron ladders clamped to the quay wall and Ron Bryce laid a plank across the gap but it was too early to go down, the well-deck was still awash. The whole forepart of the boat was decked over to form the accommodation and there was a raised wheel-house with engine controls.

Wycliffe stood with the collar of his mackintosh turned up and his hat pulled well down, apparently oblivious of the driving rain. Kersey said, 'There's no point in getting soaked. Come into the car.' Kersey's Ford Escort was parked close by.

They sat in the little car in silence and a few minutes later they were joined by Sergeant Smith with his cameras and his pipe so that they had to lower the window for ventilation. At eleven o'clock the pub closed and its customers split into two parties – one for home and bed, the other for the seamen's shelter and whatever excitement the night might bring. A quarter of an hour later Ron Bryce tapped on the car window and the policemen joined him on the quay.

'The water must be clear of the sea-cock by now, Mr Wycliffe; if you like, I'll go down and see what the damage is.'

He climbed down the ladder and sloshed about in the basin where there were still several inches of muddy water. With the help of a hand-torch he made an inspection of the hull which occupied him for three or four minutes then he called up, 'Sound as a bell, as far as I can see, Mr Wycliffe. It must be the sea-cock; shall I go aboard and shut it?'

'Is it possible to plug the drain from outside?'

'If you say so but it's easier to go aboard and shut the valve.'

'I'd rather you plugged it from outside.'

Wycliffe climbed down the ladder and stepped across the plank to stand for a moment, poised on the gunnel, then he stepped down into the well. Everything had a coat of slime; other than that and the seaweedy smell it was all surprisingly normal.

The door of the wheel-house had a brass lever-catch which shifted easily under the pressure of his finger-tip. He wanted to avoid confusing any prints which might have survived immersion. The wheel and engine controls were set on the port side and on the starboard side a couple of steps led down to the cabin-saloon.

This was it. Another door, another lever-catch which moved as easily as the first and he was looking into the saloon. The light from the flood-lamps was filtered by the glass portholes and skylight but he could see well enough. Cushions and blankets were lying in a tumbled, sodden heap on and under the long, narrow table. The locker doors had burst open, spilling their contents so that broken crockery, glasses, cans of beer, life-jackets

163

and paperbacked books were scattered all over the heap.

What did he expect? His hunch had proved right; the salvage operation had justified itself. He had reasoned correctly from the holed and drifting dinghy that someone had rowed ashore from *Manna* and that *Manna* herself had either been scuttled or she had put to sea again and gone – gone where? With only forty miles of cruising in her tanks she had vanished without trace. Well, he had the answer to that one; now the question was, who had gone ashore in the dinghy? David Clement? He had never taken that possibility seriously; it made no sort of sense. So, if Clement had been aboard *Manna* on Saturday night the chances were that he still was.

All he could see for the moment was the jumble of gear. He started to move the cushions – foam rubber, and absurdly light despite the soaking – and almost at once he saw a fawn suede shoe and the leg of a pair of fawn denim slacks . . . He moved enough of the stuff to finally satisfy himself. David Clement was aboard. David Clement was dead.

So it was on the cards that *Manna* had been scuttled to dispose of a body.

The clothing removed from the body was laid out in polythene bags on a bench in Dr Frank's laboratory. Apart from the clothing there were the contents of the pockets: loose change, a handkerchief, a ball-point pen, a disintegrating cigarette pack, a cheque-book and card, fifteen pounds in notes and two glass paperweights in their chamois leather pouches.

The naked body lay under the white light; a slight figure of a man, under five feet six inches tall, less than one hundred and thirty pounds weight. Franks, in a green surgical gown, made his examination of externals and dictated notes to his secretary, a sleepy-eyed girl, called from her bed.

The wall clock showed twenty minutes to four, the time at which human vitality seems to be at its lowest ebb. Wycliffe felt cold in the pit of his stomach and the stink of formalin nauseated him.

The features of the dead man were unrecognizable due to distortion and there were patches of greenish lividity, but where the body had been protected by clothing the changes were less marked. Mercifully the fish had been unable to reach it.

'Three or four fillings and a couple of extractions, Charles. Taken with an appendix scar about fifteen years old you should have no trouble in settling any question of identity . . .'

'What about the cause of death?' Wycliffe was impatient.

Franks was silent for some time then he said, 'There's a pretty extensive skull fracture; I'm not sure yet whether it was the actual cause of death . . . He didn't drown, if that's any help to you . . .'

Three hours later the message was the same or very nearly. 'Well, Charles, the skull fracture in the left temporal region certainly killed him; the skull was shattered with a massive internal haemorrhage.'

'A heavy blow?'

'You'd think so but you'd be wrong in this case; this chap's skull is of very uneven thickness and in this area, bordering the left squamous suture, it's thinner than any I've come across in twenty-five years of this job.'

'An egg-shell skull.'

'In that area, yes.'

'So a fall or a blow?'

Franks shook his head. 'It wouldn't have taken much of a knock but I can't answer the crunch question, fall or blow.'

'Is he healthy – *was* he healthy in other respects?'

'As far as I can tell he was a fit young man. Unfortunately he suffered a bump on the head which to anyone else would probably have caused little more than temporary discomfort, perhaps mild concussion. It could have happened to him at any time had he the ill-luck to knock himself in that particular place.'

Wycliffe was thinking of the smashed Parian figure of the naked girl lying between desk and safe in the office behind the antique shop. He said, more to himself than Franks, 'But if it was an accident there would have been no reason for all this rigmarole in disposing of the body.'

Franks grinned. 'Your side of the fence, Charles. But I agree – no more reason than to remove the weapon from the scene of a suicide.'

Wycliffe growled. 'You've got a point there.'

Franks was stripping off his gown in preparation for scrubbing himself. His secretary came in with coffee in pottery mugs.

'Sugar, Mr Wycliffe?'

'No thanks.' But he sipped the coffee and changed his mind. 'Everything in this place tastes and smells of formalin.'

He left the laboratory at a little before seven and on his way home stopped at the flat in Godolphin Street. A police watcher was in position but whether he was awake was another question. Anyway, there was no point in watching the Stokes girl now.

She came to the door in her dressing gown. 'Come in.' She led him into the little sitting-room where the curtains were still drawn. She stooped and switched on the fire then hugged her body and shivered. 'It's cold!' and then, 'I know you've got bad news.'

'We've raised *Manna*.'

'And?'

'David was aboard . . . I'm afraid he's dead.'

She sat down. 'Drowned?'

'No, the pathologist attributes death to a head injury.' He added after a moment, '*Manna* was scuttled; somebody opened the sea-cock.'

She looked up, wide-eyed, incredulous. 'You mean that David was murdered?'

'Apparently he had a very thin skull.'

'What's that got to do with it?'

'It's possible that his death was an accident – at least that he was not deliberately murdered.'

She put her hands over her face and remained still for a long time. In the end she said, 'I would like to see him.'

Wycliffe hesitated. 'There will have to be a formal identification but whether—'

She cut him short. 'I know; he's been in the water a week, but I'm a nurse.'

'I'll give you a telephone number and you can arrange it.'

She shivered again. 'We were going to live together, perhaps get married. I don't know what he really thought of me but he was the nearest I've ever come to—' She broke off, her features distorted by emotion.

Wycliffe said, 'I'm very sorry. You still can suggest no way in which all this might have come about?'

Her emotion discharged itself in a flare of temper. 'God! Don't you think I want to? There's no point in beating about the bush now. David was going to sell his boat and in a few weeks he would have pulled out. I was to join him in Bournemouth after an interval . . . I don't know what went wrong.'

They were silent for a while then he said, 'Will you be all right here on your own?'

'What? Oh, yes. You don't have to worry about me.'

It was a fine morning though mist on the horizon promised showers to come. It occurred to him that there was something wrong with the light over the estuary, then he realized that it was his internal clock that was wrong, insisting that it was evening after a night without sleep.

He felt depressed. As he saw it he had made little real

progress. Despite the fact that they had unearthed Waddington, located the motor cruiser and found David Clement he was no nearer an explanation for what had happened. And though both the Clement brothers were dead by violence he was not in a position to say that either of them had been murdered. In fact, he was becoming increasingly convinced that Joseph had shot himself. The only reason for doubt was the absence of a weapon but the idea of a double murder was scarcely credible; the brothers had died in quite different ways, and why dispose of one body and not the other?

This sort of logic left him with questions: Why had the gun been removed? How and why had David Clement died? And who was responsible? Despite his mood he grinned wryly, 'Write your answers clearly in the spaces provided.'

Helen said, 'You look all in; you're going to bed now, surely?'

'For a couple of hours.'

'I'll get lunch for one o'clock.'

'Make it twelve.'

He set the alarm because he did not altogether trust Helen to wake him. At ten minutes past twelve he telephoned his headquarters and spoke to Bourne.

'Kersey and Smith have been down at Porthellin since early this morning, sir. Mr Scales is deputizing in your office.'

He had a prickly sensation in his eyelids and a dull ache at the base of his skull but after a bath and a light lunch he felt better. At half past one he set out for Porthellin. The mist which had earlier veiled the horizon now enveloped land and sea alike, translucent and luminous. Colours were muted like soft washes in a water-colour painting and as he approached the village it seemed possessed of an air of transience and unreality. The tide was coming in, lapping round the twin keels of *Manna*; a uniformed policeman stood near the top of the iron ladder looking bored. When he spotted Wycliffe he smartened up and saluted. It was difficult to take it all seriously, the little blue and green and white boats, the pub with its lobster-pot sign, the fish-lofts which had been converted into gift shops and the cafés with their winter shutters still in place.

'No pressmen?'

The constable grinned. 'Not since the pub opened, sir.'

Kersey was in the wheel-house-chartroom of the cruiser with pub sandwiches and cans of beer. 'We've about finished here, sir. Smith has gone back to work on his stuff.'

'Has he got anything?'

'Nothing that will get us anywhere. The wheel and the engine controls have been wiped clean. This chap isn't making the kind of mistakes Smith can put on film.'

Somebody had mopped up the wheel-house and made it habitable.

'Have a beer, sir; glasses by courtesy of the owners whoever they may now be.' Kersey looked round at the white paintwork and tarnished brass. 'She's a nice craft and very well fitted out; when I come up on the pools I shall buy one like this. Esther and the girls would be over the moon.'

Wycliffe opened a can of beer and poured himself a glass. 'Any cash or valuables?'

'Not a thing.'

A gull perched on the gunnel and edged crabwise along it to peer in at the food; two more circled overhead, squawking and waking echoes in the village.

Kersey asked, 'What did Franks say?'

'Death was due to a skull injury but he had an egg-shell skull.'

'That's a fat lot of help! But however Clement died somebody thought it worth organizing that elaborate cover-up. In my opinion Lane knows something about it; I don't go for that book yarn of his. Lane went into the shop as the Ford girl says he did and, on his own showing, he was the last person we know to have seen David Clement alive.'

Wycliffe got out his pipe and started to fill it. He was still affected by a sense of unreality and found it difficult to focus his thoughts. After a little while he said, 'Who would want to kill Joseph? Conceivably his brother, though I see David as a rogue rather than a killer and, in any case, he had an alibi. In my opinion Joseph shot himself while his brother was out buying cigarettes.'

Kersey agreed. 'It looks that way, and I suppose it's possible that David didn't even know his brother was lying dead upstairs when Lane arrived.'

But Wycliffe's thoughts were following a different line; he said, 'The three of them were very close.'

Kersey looked at him, 'Sir?'

'The major, Bunny and Joe.' Wycliffe recited the three names with a half smile on his lips which puzzled Kersey. 'If Joe shot himself the other two would have blamed David.'

Kersey frowned. 'Are you saying that Lane might have roughed him up and gone further than he meant to – or something on those lines?' He broke off. 'It's an idea! And if I had my way it's an idea that would be put to Master Lane before he's much older.'

Wycliffe shook his head. 'You wouldn't get anywhere with Lane.' He added after a moment, 'I was wondering who telephoned who.'

'Telephoned?'.

'Somebody wiped the prints off the telephone and they must have had a reason. Clement would have had no reason to remove his own prints . . . ' He broke off to put a match to his pipe.

Kersey gathered up the remains of his sandwiches and threw them overboard to the waiting gulls who swooped and squawked and quarrelled out of all proportion to the prize.

Wycliffe said, 'Parkyn isn't on the phone.'

'Parkyn?' Kersey laughed. 'Plenty of people are.'

The sun broke through the mist striking answering gleams from the tarnished brasswork of the wheel-house. The tide was making rapidly now and already several of the smaller craft in the basin were afloat. The two men sat in silence for a long time; Wycliffe seemed to be absorbed in watching the shimmering reflections in the green water while Kersey sat still, holding his peace and waiting.

Wycliffe said quietly, as though continuing a train of thought, 'I've talked to Parkyn four times and he's never put a foot wrong.'

Kersey looked at him in surprise. 'You think that Parkyn—'

Wycliffe cut him off sharply. 'I think that Parkyn is playing a game with us; his whole attitude is a silent challenge. If a policeman came to see you four times on a case with which you were only marginally connected wouldn't you want to know what the hell he was after?' Wycliffe did not expect an answer and none came; he went on, 'Not Parkyn. He sits and smokes and drinks his whisky and laughs up his sleeve.'

It was rare enough for Wycliffe to air his thoughts in this way but what astonished Kersey was the uncharacteristic vein of bitterness which informed the words. He realized that Wycliffe was talking to himself rather than to him and said nothing.

'We've got to pin him down and the way to do that is to go back to the beginning. We must carry out another house-to-house in Bear Street and neighbourhood but this time we are only interested in the movements of three men: Parkyn, Lane and David Clement.' He looked straight at Kersey as though challenging him to

171

protest, 'We'll bring this out into the open and see how the major reacts then.'

Kersey was still silent but there was a shout from the quay, 'Mr Wycliffe! What about a word?' The reporters were back.

Wycliffe sighed. 'I thought I had something then but it's gone . . .'

CHAPTER NINE

Tuesday morning, with a gale from the south-west bringing squalls of rain. During the squalls the sky and sea were blue-black but the sea was flecked with crests of startling whiteness. Wycliffe breakfasted with scarcely a word to Helen and he was in his office by eight o'clock. At the cost of a restless night he had recalled what it was that had escaped him in talking over the case with Kersey – Bunny Lane had arrived at the antique shop that Saturday night *in response to a telephone call.* Although it was by no means a blinding illumination it fitted in to a more or less coherent theory which was forming in his mind, a theory which could only be put to the test by inviting confrontation. But even that might achieve no more than 'I warned you!' from Bellings and a ton of bricks from on high. However, the time had come to risk it.

Through Kersey he had arranged a special briefing session for nine o'clock.

'We are going to carry out another house-to-house inquiry in Bear Street and neighbourhood, to include Dog's Leg Lane, Garrison Drive, St John's Court and the harbour frontage. But this time we are interested in only three men – all of them well known in the district – Major Gavin Lloyd Parkyn, Michael John "Bunny" Lane, and David Clement. Your job will be to find anyone who saw these men after, say, six o'clock on Saturday evening.

'Unfortunately people's recollections are now ten days old so help them by recalling that night – the fact that it was a Saturday will mean something to most people, and remember that it was pouring with rain until late evening.'

The atmosphere in the briefing room was tense, quite unlike Wycliffe's usual sessions in which he encouraged a relaxed, conversational approach. His manner was terse and mandatory, creating a gulf between him and his listeners which could be measured by their silence.

'Any questions?'

There were none.

Back in the office Diane said, 'You know that the new duty schedules are due out on Friday—'

'Later, Diane! Get Sergeant Smith to come to my office, please.'

When Smith came a few minutes later Wycliffe's manner was equally curt.

'I want you to go back to Bear Street and look for prints or other traces which you might have missed first time round. I want that place put under a microscope. Take somebody reliable with you.'

Smith, scenting his mood, was cautious. 'You know it isn't possible to treat every surface, sir, can you suggest—'

Wycliffe cut him short. 'If I'm right, our man was waiting around, killing time, probably in the office behind the shop. Try to think what he might have done and the traces he might have left *before he had any reason to be on his guard*. Remember the exchange principle; nobody goes anywhere without leaving a trace and taking away some memento of the visit.'

Smith was nettled at being treated like a greenhorn, 'I know all about the theory, sir, but—'

Wycliffe cut him short again. 'Just try, that's what I'm asking you to do. During the morning I hope to send you a fresh set of prints for comparison purposes.'

'Is that all, sir?' Very formal.

'That's all.'

The odd thing was that he didn't feel bad tempered, only deeply preoccupied.

When Smith had gone he left the building and drove through the city, down Bear Street and up Dog's Leg Lane to Garrison Drive where the row of red-brick houses was dwarfed by the grey walls of the fort, by the great plain of the open sea, and by the menacing sky. The wind blew in tremendous gusts and his car steered uneasily. The whole place had an air of desolation, even the houses on either side of Number 3, ostentatiously cared for, looked as though their occupants had deserted them and left them to the elements.

On his way up the steep path to the house he had to brace himself against the wind in his back. Hetty opened the door, holding it with her body, and he edged his way round her into the hall. She shut the door and shot one of the bolts to stop it blowing open again. The dimly-lit hall seemed unnaturally still after the tumult outside.

'My brother is out.'

'I would like to wait for him if I may.'

She hesitated and for a moment he thought that she would make difficulties but instead she said in a voice which sounded oddly conspiratorial, 'Come with me!'

He followed her down the passage to the general's study where she opened the door and stood aside for him to enter. 'There!' She pointed to a worn leather chair by the window. 'You may wait for him in here.' She said this in the manner of one conferring a notable favour.

Hetty had changed; her movements were jerky, her eyes, which never met his, were restless, and her hair had escaped from almost all restraint so that it hung in ragged wisps about her head and even over her eyes. But the room looked much as he had first seen it – spotlessly clean and polished though now an oil-stove, less

175

odorous than others in the house, was alight and brightened the dimly-lit room with its orange glow so that it was almost cosy. And there was another change: in a corner by the fireplace a dressmaker's model was draped with the general's dress uniform. Draped was the word, for the general's bulk bore little relationship to the dimensions of the dummy which was enveloped rather than clothed, like a children's guy on firework night. But Hetty had done her best and the figure carried the general's sword and displayed his medals together with the badge and star of his Order.

'You see!' she said. 'Isn't it just like the portrait?'

She came and stood over him, hands clasped together, knuckles showing white, and he wondered what was coming next.

'Would you like a cup of coffee?'

A reflex refusal was stifled just in time. 'Thank you, I would.'

She went out, leaving the door wide open.

Presumably, despite the weather, the major was doing his daily round – the newsagent, the betting shop, the butcher . . . The roar of the wind was subdued by the stout walls and the back of the house was to some extent sheltered, but now and then a more powerful gust made the whole building shudder and fragments of plaster rattled down the chimney into the empty grate.

He could hear Hetty moving about in the kitchen and ten minutes later she came in with a tray, two chipped pottery mugs, a jug of coffee, milk and a bowl of sugar.

'Black or white? . . . Do you take sugar?'

It was incredible.

When the coffee had been poured and she was holding her mug in both hands as though to warm them, she said, 'Have you come to arrest Gavin?'

'Arrest him? Of course not! Why do you ask that?'

She smiled a bleak little smile. 'I am not a fool, Mr Wycliffe. I listened to what you told him on Sunday. I have to listen at keyholes or I should hear nothing.' She sipped her coffee, her eyes on him. 'You told him what happened in that antique shop and how the boat was taken round to Porthellin and sunk in the bay and how somebody rowed ashore in the little dinghy . . . ' She paused for a while then added, 'It was obvious you suspected Gavin and now, since then, you've got the boat up and found another dead man. I heard that on the wireless.'

Wycliffe said nothing.

Hetty, taking her coffee mug with her, walked over to the fireplace where she stood with her back to Wycliffe looking up at her father's portrait. 'When you arrest someone do they have to be put on trial?'

'Anyone charged with a crime has to appear in court—'

'Even if they confess?'

'Confession to the police is not accepted as proof of guilt, but you really must not jump to—'

She turned to face him abruptly and put her finger to her lips enjoining silence in a childish gesture. 'Sh!'

There were sounds of a door opening and closing, a man's cough . . .

'Here he is!' She hurried out of the room with the tray.

Parkyn came to the door. 'Ah, Wycliffe! A wild day!' His face was flushed by the wind. 'Come to my room.'

'No! Let him say what he has to say here.' Hetty was standing behind her brother, hidden by his bulk.

The major turned slowly to face her and looked at her for several seconds without a word, then he said, 'This way, Wycliffe.'

It was the first time he had been a witness to open hostility between them and the first time he had seen Hetty quelled.

In Parkyn's little room the inevitable heater was already burning, giving off its clammy warmth. Parkyn stooped to the cupboard and came up with his tray – whisky, carafe, glasses . . .

'Will you join me?'

'Not just now.'

Wycliffe's visits were already acquiring a ritual character and the fact was not lost on the major who greeted his reply with a sardonic smile. He poured himself a half-tumbler of whisky and added a little water.

'Sit down, Wycliffe.'

Parkyn lowered himself into his own chair in which the worn upholstery, devoid of all pattern and texture, had moulded itself to his form. He stretched out his legs to the heater; his trousers were soaked to the knees. A gulp of whisky was followed by the ritual sigh. 'Well, what is it this time?'

'I suppose you've heard that Clement's boat has been raised and that we found his body in the cabin?'

'Yes, I heard that. How did he die? Was he drowned?'

'No, he died of a fractured skull which caused a severe brain haemorrhage.'

Parkyn was holding his glass to the light, apparently studying the clarity of the whisky. 'A blow?'

'Possibly. The pathologist tells me that he had what is known as an "egg-shell" skull.'

Parkyn balanced his glass on the arm of his chair. 'Ah! I've known such a case; a man in our unit knocked his head against the vaulting-horse during a training session and his skull seemed to collapse. Of course, that was an accident.'

'So might this have been, but it could have been manslaughter or even murder.'

Parkyn shook his head. 'A murderer could hardly be expected to have knowledge of the thickness of his victim's skull.' He got out his pipe and pouch. 'Smoke?'

'I won't smoke now, thank you.'

The major's back was to the door but Wycliffe was sitting side-on and he could see that the door was very slightly ajar though he felt sure that Parkyn had closed it. No doubt Hetty was listening.

Wycliffe said, 'I wonder if you telephoned Bunny Lane before or after David Clement died?'

Parkyn was filling his pipe but he looked up with one of those faint smiles which was no more than a twitch of the lip.

An unmistakable creak came from the passage and Wycliffe was surprised that Parkyn either had not heard it or chose to ignore it. He had filled his pipe and was going through the ritual of lighting it. Between puffs he said, 'Why did you come here this morning, Wycliffe?' His manner was unconcerned, casually curious.

More than once in the past few days Wycliffe had thought that he was allowing himself to be intimidated by this larger-than-life character whose peace of mind, according to Bellings, was still of concern in high places. Would he have behaved to any other suspect as he had behaved – was behaving, with Parkyn? In any case he had decided on confrontation.

'I want you to be quite clear about where you stand.'

The prominent eyes widened. 'Ah!'

Wycliffe followed up with a request which he had intended to put with greater subtlety. 'There is something else; you are under no obligation at this stage but I would like you to have your fingerprints taken for purposes of comparison.'

'Isn't it usual to say for purposes of elimination?'

Wycliffe said, 'If you will come with me to Mallet Street police station it will only take a few minutes and I will bring you straight back.'

Parkyn removed his pipe from his mouth. 'No, Wycliffe. I am not going to any police station and I will have no truck with your little inky pads, but if you want my prints you can have them.' He lifted up the whisky bottle which was almost empty and drained it into his glass, then he offered it to Wycliffe. 'There, that should do you . . . Wait a minute . . .'

He heaved himself out of his chair and went to his

desk where he found a crumpled carrier-bag. He dropped the bottle in the bag. 'There! That will keep the rain off.'

Parkyn came with him to the door and stood on the steps, in front of the closed door, while Wycliffe fought his way down the garden in the very teeth of the gale, clutching his carrier-bag.

Seated at the wheel of his car, he swore. He was in no doubt about who had come off best in that round. But the defeat was moral, not professional. He was not disappointed. With Parkyn's temperament and experience it was unlikely that he would make the mistake of saying too much and, in fact, he had said almost nothing. But Hetty had talked; so much so that he was uneasy. Hetty was convinced that it was only a matter of time before her brother's arrest. 'When you arrest someone do they have to be put on trial? . . . Even if they confess?'

It was the threat of disgrace to the saintly and gallant general's memory which troubled Hetty.

Wycliffe parked his car by the old custom-house and walked up Bear Street to the antique shop. There were few people about and in one place a swirling mass of brown water extended half-way across the road where a drain had become blocked. He handed over the major's whisky bottle to Smith whose manner was even more withdrawn and morose than usual.

'Anything fresh?'

'No, sir.'

Annie was serving lunches so he crossed the street and took his seat at one of the tables. While he was eating he realized that he was being pointed out by the knowing regulars to others not so knowing.

Afterwards he returned to headquarters and to his office. It was still raining and even through the hermetically sealed double-glazing he could hear it lashing against the glass.

Diane came in. 'Mr Bellings has been asking to see

you; he would like you to go along to his office when it is convenient.'

Diane was stiff and formal, still responding to his manner of the morning.

'I'll go now.'

She looked at him in surprise at his ready compliance. The truth was that he felt himself to be in some sort of limbo – waiting and hoping that something decisive would turn up before a fresh wave of publicity caught up with the case and the press started handing out cod about a possible security angle. It would come. Sooner or later a bright reporter would spot his interest in Parkyn, do his homework, and then the gentlemen from Millbank really would get interested.

He walked down the main corridor, through the sacred door and into the carpeted precincts. Bellings's personal assistant said, 'Go straight in, Mr Wycliffe. Mr Bellings is expecting you.'

'Oh, Charles! Nice of you to find the time.' A hint of sarcasm? Who could tell?

The reason for the interview was soon apparent; Bellings had chosen this moment to tell him of his impending departure.

'A chance I can't afford to miss, Charles! A lectureship in criminology is the sort of pipe-dream one has but never expects to realize ... You and the chief have always looked on me as a too academic policeman and, here I am, proving you right.'

Bellings's words were, as always, accompanied by restrained though expressive gestures with his long, aesthetic hands. He punctuated what he had to say with precisely calculated pauses and, at the right moment, he would catch the eye of his listener with a deprecatory smile. Wycliffe thought, He can't fail to be a hit with his students; especially the women.

Bellings went on to indulge in elegant nostalgia with a discreet measure of self-denigration, rounded off with a few well-turned phrases expressing thanks and appreciation of 'your unfailing support and co-operation . . .'

Wycliffe put it down as a well-rehearsed performance and acknowledged it as graciously as he was able. At the same time he had been taking stock of the deputy's office which, if he said 'Yes' on Wednesday evening, might be his. The office was little different from his own, a little more plush, and it looked out over the car-park instead of the highway; but beyond the car-park there were real fields with cows and trees. True, the developers and planners had their beady eyes on that land but the conservationist lobby was learning the tricks of the trade and becoming almost as devious as the opposition. Not that he would be influenced by the view, it was that padded door which swished shut behind one – a symbol.

Bellings was looking at him as though he expected something. 'Well, that's it, Charles; the end of a chapter for me! I start afresh with the Michaelmas Term in October.'

'Yes, yes, I see . . .' Wycliffe's thoughts had wandered and he was a little at a loss so that he changed the subject with unflattering abruptness. 'You were telling me the other day about Parkyn's career and his reputation; I wonder if you could tell me a bit more about him as a man?'

Belling's expression froze. He would have liked to refuse but he hesitated to put himself in the position of withholding information from a colleague on police business. He spread his pale hands in a helpless gesture. 'What, exactly, do you want to know?'

'His temperament; the kind of man he is?'

Bellings answered tight-lipped, 'I've already told you that my direct knowledge of Parkyn comes from a brief spell of service with him in Korea – a few months only, when we were both very young men . . .' He paused to allow the point to sink in and give himself time to think.

'I have told you that he was the sort of man who seemed to put himself at risk as a matter of deliberate choice – he didn't wait until he found himself in a tight corner, he sought out such situations. He trailed his coat, as the Irish say. Or so it seemed to me and to others who knew him at the time.

'There was no question of going hunting or histrionics, he was always extremely taciturn about his exploits, often aggressively so, and it sometimes seemed to me that he was ashamed of this wild streak in his nature.'

Bellings picked up a slim, expensive ball-point and played with it. (Wycliffe had been given a similar one for Christmas but preferred a Staedtler Stick).

'He seemed to be driven, as I believe some men are, constantly to challenge fate – to hazard himself.' Bellings added, with more insight than Wycliffe would have given him credit for, 'I have thought since that such men may feel menaced by fear – the fear of being afraid and so they put themselves to endless tests . . . '

'And socially? How did he get on with his companions?'

Another frown and a caustic aside. 'The conditions were hardly conducive to an elaborate social life. However, Parkyn was as self-effacing as a man of his bulk could be but the truth is that he didn't fit in terribly well. At that time he didn't drink or smoke and he detested sport . . . Of course, nobody had any idea then of his potential . . . '

Bellings would not have been flattered had he realized that Wycliffe was matching this assessment with that of Parkyn's bookie and finding, on the whole, that they made a good marriage.

Wycliffe was going though the case-file. At a certain stage in an investigation he would spend time browsing through the records which, for the most part, were as exciting as last week's news, but there was a chance that something, passed over at the time as trivial, might now have importance.

The telephone rang – Smith, his manner a mixture of satisfaction and lingering resentment, 'I've found a set of prints which seem to match those you brought me. I'm speaking from the antique shop but I propose coming back to do a proper comparison. The prints – index, second and third fingers of the right hand – were on the underside of the lavatory seat in the downstairs cloak-room.'

Wycliffe heaved a sigh. It was no absolute break-through, there was nothing to say how long the prints had been there – but it was a sign, like Noah's dove returning with an olive leaf in her beak.

He turned again to his file, in particular to a packet of photographs labelled with a series of index numbers; photographs taken by Smith of Joseph's room after the removal of the body but before it was disturbed by the searchers. Smith was a good photographer; every detail stood out clearly and, taken together, the photographs made an almost complete record of the room without need of written report. Wycliffe spread them on his desk.

Joseph's bed – a single bed with a crumpled beds-pread; even in the photograph it looked grubby. Over the bed Joseph kept his books on makeshift shelving; books on furniture and on stamps. It was possible to read the titles on many of them. Another photograph showed the top of the desk; a loose-leafed album with quadrille rulings open at a page labelled, *Guatemala: Quetzal Design of 1879*, in careful italic script. The tools of his hobby were there: forceps, magnifier, perforation gauge . . . a few stamps in polythene envelopes. Then there was a large china ashtray, a willow-patterned tobacco jar and the pipe he had, presumably, been smoking was laid down by the album. There was a glass pen-tray with ball-points and pencils and an old-fashioned stub-nibbed pen for writing the headings in his albums.

Wycliffe turned to another of Smith's studies – for that is what they were – showing the wall to the right of the desk where there was a picture, a dim oil-painting in a gilt frame, and below it a rack of Joseph's pipes, more than a dozen of them, all of similar pattern with small, squat bowls and long, slender stems. Interesting, a man's choice of pipes; what did these tell one about Joseph? That despite his apparent sturdy stolidity there was a finer, aesthetic side to his nature? Parkyn, too, went in for long-stemmed pipes but preferred a bigger, deeper bowl giving a longer smoke. Parkyn's pipes were similar to Wycliffe's own. And Bunny Lane? Bunny stuck to the relatively short stem and stout bowl of the honest tradesman, ignoring the fact that the species had all but disappeared with Stanley Baldwin.

The internal telephone buzzed and he depressed a key. 'Sergeant Kersey to see you, Mr Wycliffe.'

'Send him in.'

Kersey came in, glanced at the photographs spread on the desk, and said with a grin, 'English interiors of the late twentieth-century Smith school. I recognize the technique.'

'You've got something?'

'Something. D.C. Edwards, on house-to-house, has just reported in. I don't know if you remember, but in Dog's Leg Lane, on the right-hand side, just below the bend there's a house with a little window low down, almost level with the street. An old couple called Poat have lived there since way back and on Saturday evening, when it was raining like a flood, the drain choked outside and they had water coming into their kitchen. Old Poat had to go out and clear it and while he was at it Parkyn went by.'

'What time was this?'

'A bit before eight.' Kersey went on. 'The odd thing is,

the major didn't go down the hill towards Bear Street but turned off along the alley which runs behind the houses.'

Wycliffe said, 'The Ford girl!'

Kersey nodded. 'It's the only answer. My mother used to say God puts at least one surprise in every packet and she was dead right.'

Wycliffe said, 'Go and talk to her.'

When Kersey rang the bell he could hear a vacuum cleaner at work and when Marilyn opened the door she was wearing an overall with a scarf round her head.

'Afternoon, Marilyn. Cleaning up?'

She looked at him with a suspicious air. 'I thought we'd lost you. Didn't you get promoted or something?'

'Or something. Can I come in?'

She stood aside. 'You will anyway. Have you come for my statement?'

Kersey went into the candy-floss room, lifted a satin doll off one of the armchairs and sat down. The vacuum cleaner stood in the middle of the floor. It was like seeing a night-club in the cold light of day.

'Make yourself at home.'

'Thanks.' Kersey was manipulating the limbs of the doll into grotesque attitudes which made the plump girl laugh.

'I thought I knew all your regulars, Marilyn.'

She stopped laughing. 'You cops think you know everything.'

'Major Gavin Lloyd Parkyn, R.M., C.B.E., D.S.O. etc., etc . . .'

'I don't know what you're talking about.'

'Not what, who. His father was a "Sir" and a general and he's been quite a nob in his day. You're moving up in the world, love.'

'What do you want?'

'A week ago last Saturday, at a little before nine, you

186

heard a shot; later, you saw a man come up the street and go into the antique shop. That's what you told my boss.'

'It's true.'

'Yes, but what you didn't tell him was that Parkyn was with you until a few minutes before you heard the shot. How long, exactly?'

'If he wasn't here, I can't tell you how long it was before he left, can I?' She pulled off the scarf from round her head and released a great bouncy mass of dark curls as though in defiance.

Kersey wagged his finger at her. 'Naughty! We know he was here; you won't do yourself any good by lying about it. How long before the shot did he leave?'

She turned to the vacuum cleaner and seemed about to switch it on. 'You're hindering me in my work.' It was a half-hearted tactic; she had had too many dealings with the police to believe that she could get away with it.

Kersey remained good humoured. 'And you know that I shall hinder you a hell of a lot more if you don't tell me what I want to know.'

'You can't make me answer questions; I don't do anything against the law.'

'Who said you did? But one of my lads spending the odd evening now and again lounging about in your alley would scare your clients away for weeks.'

'You're a real bastard!' But she said it without heat. 'Less than five minutes.'

'Five minutes or less after Parkyn left you heard the shot; is that it?'

'About that. Of course, as I told your boss I didn't realize it was a shot then.' She looked at him, suddenly wide-eyed. 'You're not saying that he—'

'How long has Parkyn been coming here?'

'A long time; probably a couple of years, perhaps more, but it's ridiculous for you—'

'How often?'

'Usually Wednesdays and Saturdays.'

'How do you get on with him?'

'That's what I'm trying to tell you. He's real nice; I only wish there was more like him; he wouldn't hurt a fly.'

'One of those who come mainly for the chat, is that it?'

'What's that got to do with you?'

'All right, was he his usual cheery, chatty self on Saturday evening?'

'I didn't see any difference; he's always pleasant which is more than I can say for some.'

'Has he been here since?'

'As usual.'

Kersey tried again. 'Has he mentioned the Clement brothers or what happened over there?'

'He never talks about other people; he's no gossip.'

'You should write him a testimonial. Which way did he leave?'

'There's only one way out of here – down the stairs.'

Kersey's manner hardened. 'Don't be funny with me, girl! I'm not joking about queering your pitch. Which way?'

'You know most of 'em go and come the back way.'

'And Parkyn that Saturday night?'

She hesitated. 'I think he went out the front way, I thought I heard his footsteps in the street but I couldn't say for sure.'

'Come off it! You went to the window, didn't you?'

She gave up. 'All right, I saw him. When I looked out he was on the opposite pavement talking to the younger brother from the antique shop.'

'You mean he'd knocked at the door or something?'

'I don't think so. I think they'd just happened to meet there; that's what it looked like.'

'And?'

'And nothing. My telephone rang and I went out into the passage to answer it. I wasn't on the phone more than a couple of minutes and it was when I came back in here that I heard the bang.'

Kersey stood up and replaced the doll on the chair. She watched him, apprehensive, 'I hope he's not going to be in trouble.'

Kersey said, 'You want to watch out, my girl! When you start worrying about other people it's a bad sign.'

'Bastard!'

Before he had closed the door behind him he heard the vacuum cleaner start up again.

Wycliffe went back to his photographs and wondered what he had been thinking about before Kersey interrupted. Pipes – that was it; nothing worth remembering. He was about to gather up the photographs and return them to their envelope when his eye was caught again by the one of Joseph's desk. It showed the album with his stamp gear, the tobacco jar and ashtray – and the pipe. The pipe lay beside the stamp album as though it had been one of Joseph's last acts to place it there before . . . But the pipe was not like the others in the rack on the wall. It had a long stem like them but a heavier, deeper bowl.

It must have been the estimable Poirot who said, '*Mon ami*, a clue two feet long is every bit as valuable as one measuring two millimetres.' One up to the little Belgian's grey cells. Criminal investigation is apt to get bogged down by minutiae. Well, the pipe on the desk was not two feet long but it was big enough to have been overlooked.

He spoke to D.C. Trice on the telephone. In addition to being responsible for scene-of-crime inventories she was also custodian of the stuff recorded. When the police handed back premises to the owners it was her job to deal with suspicious relatives wanting to know what had happened to aunty's butterfly-wing brooch or granny's silver bracelet.

189

'Yes, sir. There was a pipe in the pocket of the jacket Joseph was wearing – half smoked . . . I'm not an authority on pipes but this one had a small, squat bowl, a long stem and a broad mouth-piece . . . '

'Listen! I want you to go to the flat, to Joseph's room, and collect the pipe you will find lying on his desk next to the open stamp album. Hand it over to Sergeant Smith for prints. If he doesn't find any identifiable prints there is still the "bite" which is nearly as distinctive . . . '

Kersey came in looking moderately pleased with himself. 'I think we've pretty well nailed him this time, sir. We've got a witness prepared to say that he was outside the antique shop, talking to David Clement, within a minute or two of nine o'clock.' He told his story. 'Parkyn must have run into David as he was leaving the house to buy his cigarettes.'

Wycliffe said, 'I think we may have another witness to say that he went inside.' He held out Smith's photograph and pointed to the pipe lying beside the open album.

Kersey frowned. 'I don't get it.'

'That pipe is not like the ones in the rack on the wall but it *is* like the pipes Parkyn smokes.'

Kersey, a non pipe smoker, looked dubious. 'You think he left it behind?'

Wycliffe was sitting back in his chair looking dreamily at the litter of photographs on his desk. 'It's not difficult to imagine. You've just said that Parkyn ran into David as he was leaving the house. Presumably Parkyn said he'd come to see Joseph and David told him that Joseph was up in his room. "You can go on up." On the stairs, or in the corridor upstairs, Parkyn heard the shot and rushed into Joe's room to find him collapsed on the floor by the desk. Parkyn was carrying a pipe in his hand – I often do when I go into someone else's house – he dropped it on the desk while he knelt down to see what could be done for Joe . . . '

Kersey screwed up his features into one of his famous grimaces. 'And forgot about it! I wonder if he remembered it afterwards. Is it still there?'

'I've sent Liz Trice to collect it and take it to Smithy.'

Kersey scratched his chin. 'To think that it's been there under our noses from the start . . .'

CHAPTER TEN

The telephone rang. 'Wycliffe.'

Information Room with a report of a fire at Number 3, Garrison Drive. 'Knowing your interest in the premises, sir . . . '

Wycliffe swore. 'I'm going to Garrison Drive, Diane. Find Kersey and tell him to join me there.'

The rain had stopped but he drove through the streets which were still streaming with water and every vehicle carried with it a plume of spray. In Bear Street men in orange jackets languidly organized chaos round the blocked drain but he got through to the turn-off for Dog's Leg Lane. As he topped the rise and came out into the open, there was the bay a vast cauldron of white foam, and the air was misty with driven spray. Helen would be worried about salt-burn on her camellias.

From the house in Garrison Drive a ragged plume of dense black smoke like a fox's brush was being whipped inland.

There was a fire tender, two ambulances and a police car parked in the road; hoses snaked up through the garden of Number 3. He could see smoky orange flames flicking upwards from the back of the house, possibly from the general's study or the room above. Luckily the Victorians had not been miserly with space, there was a thirty-foot gap between the houses.

A young fire officer was talking on the radio in the cab of the tender; he recognized Wycliffe and came down. 'I've got another appliance round the back but the fire has a strong hold.'

'The occupants – a man and his sister – what happened to them?'

'Both have burns – the woman quite bad burns it seems. The brother got his fishing her out of the room where the fire started, downstairs at the back. I gather there was an oil-stove overturned.' The young man treated Wycliffe to a canny look. 'Is there something I should know about all this?'

Wycliffe said, 'I'm interested in these people; it's possible there may be a forensic angle.'

There was a sound of splintering wood and myriads of sparks shot up above the house and tore off on the wind.

'That'll be the floor of the room above, now it won't be long before the roof timbers are alight. I'd better get back up there.'

The ambulance men were coming down the garden of the next-door house carrying a stretcher between them. A uniformed constable walked beside them. The stretcher was put into the first ambulance and Wycliffe had a glimpse of Hetty's face, unnaturally pale but composed. Was she unconscious? A man got in beside her and the ambulance moved off.

'How is she?'

The constable answered. 'Quite badly burned about the legs, sir, but they seem to think she'll make it.'

'And the brother?'

'They're seeing to him now. His hands and arms caught it, dragging her out. He'll go in the other ambulance; they didn't want to keep his sister waiting.'

A few minutes later two other ambulance men came down the garden, one of them carrying a folded stretcher. Parkyn walked with them, evidently refusing to be a stretcher case; his arms and hands were smothered with bandages and he wore his old duffle coat draped over his shoulders and held there by a loop of string. His eyes lighted on Wycliffe and he grinned briefly. 'I've heard it said that there's no show without Punch.'

He steadied himself against the corner of the ambulance. 'It was the heater in the old man's room; she must have knocked the damn thing over.' With a sigh of resignation he allowed himself to be guided into the ambulance.

'Where are they being taken?'

'Casualty at County General. The woman may be transferred to a burns unit.'

'Will the man be kept in?'

'At his age with second-degree burns and shock they won't let him go for a day or two.'

Kersey arrived and found Wycliffe at the back of the house surveying a random collection of furniture and other belongings which had been rescued from the house and now lay half-buried in the wilderness of the garden.

'You'd better stay here. Get hold of the social services people and ask them to make arrangements for this stuff to be stored. I want a police watch on the place until forensic have had a look at it; not that what they say will make any difference but we must go by the book.'

Half the house had been destroyed and the fire was still not out though more or less under control. There was a great gap in the roof and flames still licked round the carbonized rafters.

Kersey said, 'You think it was an accident?'

Wycliffe snapped. 'Of course it wasn't! If I'd had any sense I should have expected something of the sort.' He looked up at the still burning house. 'The woman is obsessed; this is a belated funeral pyre for the old general, a sort of time-lapse suttee . . . ' He smiled with a certain bitterness. 'But Gavin fished her out and spoiled it.' He looked round him in a vague way then braced himself, 'Anyway, I'm off!'

194

He drove back to his office. The streets were no longer like rivers and the wind was dropping. He put in half-an-hour at his desk on the day's paperwork.

People were going home, the bulding was emptying. He stood by his window watching the homeward traffic. Everything had been washed clean and overhead the clouds were parting leaving a great rift of blue. He was tempted to call on Bunny Lane but he wanted to talk to the major first. At six-fifteen he went down to the canteen where he was an infrequent visitor. Sausages, bacon and fried bread – the kind of meal likely to benefit only the police pension fund; afterwards he drank two cups of canteen coffee. He smoked a pipe while chatting to a colleague from Traffic and it was seven o'clock when he returned to his office.

He picked up the telephone and asked for the casualty department at County General. Hospitals are not fond of policemen, they suspect them of having designs on their patients, which they often have.

'Casualty Sister . . . Yes, we have had a Gavin Lloyd Parkyn in casualty . . . We applied dressings and administered a sedative . . . He was not admitted to any ward . . . Certainly he should have been but he refused admission and took himself off . . . Of course it was stupid – an oldish man suffering from second-degree burns and shock needs professional attention but there was nothing we could do about it. I have enough problems looking after the people who want what we have to offer them . . . Our receptionist called a taxi and one of my nurses saw him into it . . . I've no idea; you'd better speak to the receptionist. I'll have this call transferred.'

The receptionist told him that she had phoned Radio Taxis who had an office just round the corner from the hospital and that Parkyn had left in one of their taxis at just before six-thirty.

Wycliffe had no doubt where the major would have made for and phoned Bunny Lane.

Lane said, 'I haven't seen him, Mr Wycliffe. Is there something wrong?'

Wycliffe told him. Bunny had heard nothing of the fire.

Wycliffe then spoke to the taxi firm: 'One of your chaps picked up a fare from casualty at County General at a little before six-thirty this evening . . .'

They agreed to trace the cab and ring back.

Kersey telephoned. The fire at Garrison Drive was out but a fire appliance was standing by. Kersey had arranged for a police guard and no examination of the ruin would be possible until mid-day tomorrow.

He had no sooner finished with Kersey than the taxi people were back on the line. 'Our driver has just delivered the fare to a house in St John's Court. The delay was due to the fact that your man stopped at three public houses on the way, telling the driver to wait. He came out of the last one carrying a bottle of whisky.'

Wycliffe drove through the city; the streets were quiet and so were the elements after a tempestuous day. Cotton wool clouds drifted across the sky. He parked, probably for the last time in this routine, outside the old custom-house and walked to St John's Court.

Never in twenty-five years of C.I.D. work had he found himself nearing the end of a case with so little idea of how it would turn out. It had been not so much a case as a battle of wits. He had very little doubt now about what had happened but much depended on interpretation and, in particular, on the framing of the charges. For the two men concerned that could make the difference between a longish spell in prison and a suspended sentence. The prudent course for Wycliffe would be to steer clear – prefer a holding charge and leave the rest to the police lawyers, but he was rarely prudent in his own interest.

His feelings must not enter into it but they inevitably would. The major and Bunny had taken the law into their own hands – a heinous crime. Far safer to bash an old lady over the head and run off with her handbag. British justice abhors private enterprise but Wycliffe did not always share that view. And at the back of his mind was the uncomfortable feeling that in pursuing the case he had also pursued a personal end though he would have had difficulty in saying what that end was.

There was a light showing through the fanlight over Bunny Lane's front door. Wycliffe knocked and almost at once there were footsteps in the stone passage and Bunny opened the door. He seemed relieved.

'Mr Wycliffe! Come in, let me take your coat.' He added in a lower tone, 'He's here and I'm very worried about him.'

The room looked just as it had done when, a few nights earlier, he had played dominoes with the major and Bunny; the box of dominoes still stood in the middle of the big square table. A fire burned in the grate and the major was seated in his usual chair, a bottle of whisky and a jug of water at his elbow. His arms were bandaged and the left was in a sling but his right arm was free and in that hand he held a glass of whisky, half-full. His cheeks were unnaturally flushed, his eyes seemed more prominent and his breathing was loud and laboured. But he greeted Wycliffe with his customary sardonic smile.

'You didn't waste much time, Wycliffe!'

Bunny said, 'The major arrived here twenty minutes ago.'

Wycliffe turned to the major. 'You should be in hospital.'

Parkyn took a mouthful of whisky, swallowed it, and clumsily wiped his mouth with the side of his hand. 'I prefer it here.' He added after a moment, 'Bunny telephoned to ask about Hetty. They say she's as well as can be expected, whatever that means.' He turned in his chair to face Wycliffe and winced at an unexpected

197

aggravation of his pain. 'I suppose you realize that she tried to burn herself alive in there with the old man's bits and pieces?' He sighed. 'I never knew she felt that deeply about it all . . . Think of it!' He turned away. 'No right to push her that far . . . '

Wycliffe thought, 'Poor Hetty! Now she owes him her life and she'll never forgive him for that.'

Once more the room seemed to dictate its own pace, its own silences, as the clink-clink of the little clock chased the seconds away. The major's breathing maintained an uncertain rhythm with breaks which caused the two men to look anxiously at his flushed features.

The gravelly voice resumed. 'Hetty was always a strange girl. She should have been a man; that's been her trouble all along. She's never forgiven me for being one and not making a better job of it.' He grinned unexpectedly, 'My God, if she had been, the army would have had to look out!'

He turned again to Wycliffe with a sheepish expression. 'If she gets over this, let her tell her own story – eh? Give her own version. No need to put words into her mouth . . . I mean, she might not want to admit . . . ' He broke off once more and when he spoke again he was on another tack. 'She couldn't bear the thought of me coming up before the courts over this affair and letting the old man down.' He laughed briefly. 'That's what I've been doing for most of my life according to her – letting the old man down.'

Another mouthful of whisky, another sigh. 'Well, I don't think she need worry now.'

Bunny Lane was watching him with the concern of a mother for her child. 'He shouldn't be drinking like that . . . His heart—'

The major cut him short. 'Don't be such an old woman, Bunny!'

Lane said, 'I think we should call MacDonald.

MacDonald is his doctor – he's under treatment for heart trouble.'

'You can call MacDonald or you can call the bloody undertaker when I've said what I want to say to Wycliffe but not before!' He made an effort to ease himself into a more comfortable position. 'You realize, Wycliffe, that Joe shot himself because of the antics of that bastard brother of his?'

Wycliffe nodded.

'I was on the stairs ... I heard the shot. Another minute and I could have saved him ... The brother was out, I'd just left him in the street.' His voice failed him and he breathed heavily for a while, then he took another drink.

'Am I the only one drinking? What are you thinking about, Bunny? Is Wycliffe a teetotaller?'

Bunny looked at Wycliffe, anxious, questioning, and Wycliffe nodded. Bunny got up and left the room.

The major followed him with his eyes. 'Good chap ... Salt of the earth. Try and make it easy for him ... My fault; imposed on his loyalty ... Never been able to resist the chance to cock a snook.'

Wycliffe said quietly, 'At what?'

The major frowned. 'Fate, I suppose. What else?'

'You are a fatalist?'

'Dyed in the wool. I've always taken a fatalistic view of life and that means that I was bound to see myself as impotent.' He laughed then winced at the pain. 'My reason tells me that, but the rest of me resents it like hell.'

'And so?'

An irritable gesture. 'And so me! A contradiction – isn't that what we all are? Nothing at all, pretending to be something.'

Bunny came back with the inevitable tin tray, the bottle of white wine and the highly polished glasses. He put the tray on a low stool, removed the cork which had already been drawn and looked at Wycliffe.

'Thanks.'

As well be hung for a sheep as a lamb. Wycliffe's proper course was to insist on a medical opinion but he needed no doctor to tell him that the major was a very sick man.

Bunny poured two glasses of wine and passed one to Wycliffe, then before sitting down, he put several lumps of coal on the fire. With an effort the major poured himself some more whisky and added a dash of water.

'Your very good health, gentlemen!' He drank deeply. A long-drawn-out sigh and the heavy, more or less regular breathing resumed. The major was gazing into the fire, motionless except for the heaving movements of his chest. The other two waited for him to speak and when he did his voice and manner were set in the low key of reminiscence.

'There was nothing to be done for Joe – half of one side of his face .. I went down to the office and telephoned Bunny then I waited for the brother to come back. When he did I showed him what he was responsible for – *what he had done.*'

The major's manner was grim and Wycliffe had never been more conscious of the power of the man.

'He didn't say much but his attitude was callous – indifferent. I said my piece and he became offensive. By that time we were back downstairs with the intention of phoning the police.' The major's voice strengthened, 'It was then that he made a remark which angered me and I hit him . . .'

The silence which followed lasted so long that Wycliffe wondered if Parkyn had said all he intended or was able to say. His breathing had become shallower and his cheeks seemed to have lost something of their unnatural colour. He raised his glass to his lips but changed his mind and did not drink. When he spoke again he made a couple of false starts before his voice found its usual register.

'I hit him only once and he went down. On the way he struck his head against the corner of the desk and knocked over the little figure of a naked woman which stood there . . . Somehow he cracked his skull. You tell me he had a thin place; anyway, he never moved again.'

The major drew a deep breath, raised his glass to his lips once more and this time he drank deeply. The whisky must have entered his air passages for he began to cough; a great spasm of coughing shook his whole body. Lane took the glass from his hand but he and Wycliffe could only look on helplessly while the major's body was racked convulsively. The fit lasted a couple of minutes then subsided, leaving him red-faced and gasping, but after a little while he recovered.

'Sorry! . . . Went the wrong way . . . ' He reached for the glass which Lane had taken from his hand and sipped slowly. 'Ah! that's better! . . . Much better! . . . As I was saying, he was dead. I hadn't intended to do him an injury, merely to chastise him, but there it was . . . I can't pretend that I felt greatly distressed; I've seen too many better men die for no reason at all in war and he was a rat!'

Once more silence took possession of the room broken only by the ticking of the clock and the major's laborious breathing. It might have been expected that Wycliffe would have questioned the two men but he sat as they did, staring into the fire without a word.

After a time the major's breathing became easier and he resumed where he had left off. 'It was about then that Bunny arrived. I let him in through the shop. Of course he didn't know about the younger brother and it came as a shock . . . ' The major was speaking in short phrases separated by long intervals, partly because of difficulties with his breathing but also because his manner was once more reflective and he seemed to be speaking as much to himself as to Wycliffe. Then his voice strengthened and became more incisive, 'I decided not to call the police.' He turned painfully until he was facing Wycliffe. 'If the bastard had lived I would have made it my business to expose him as a cheap crook; now that he was dead he should be known for what, in my view, he was – a murderer.'

Another long period of silence during which the little clock chivvied the seconds away.

'He had killed Joe as surely as if he had pulled the trigger ... The scheme was simple enough; David Clement would disappear with his boat and it would seem that he had cleared out after killing his brother. All that was necessary was to remove the weapon and dispose of the boat and the body. I saw no injustice in that – neither do I now ... ' His voice faltered and he added, 'But it was irresponsible, and in terms of its effect on Hetty it was damnable.'

Perhaps it was ironic to hear a man who had so recently affirmed his fatalism talking of motives and laying claim to guilt but that was not how it seemed to Wycliffe at the time.

The major took a gulp of whisky and once more started to cough. This time the glass slid out of his hand and rolled off his lap to the floor before anyone could catch it. The paroxysms were worse and they followed each other more quickly so that he had no time for more than an occasional wheezing inhalation before he was seized with another spasm. Then, quite suddenly, the coughing stopped, the major's body ceased to heave, and he was still.

Bunny said in a hushed voice, 'He's gone!'

Wycliffe bent over the motionless body.

Bunny said, 'I'll phone MacDonald.'

After he had telephoned the two men sat waiting. Outwardly nothing had changed. Daylight had faded imperceptibly so that the only light in the room now came from the fire. Bunny got up, switched on the light, then, like a prudent housekeeper, drew the curtains.

Bunny's voice was uncertain as he said, 'When he arrived he'd already had quite a few and he brought a full bottle with him. He just sat there and drank and there was nothing I could do ... ' His eyes were glistening with tears. 'He told me how he got his burns and he said, "Our friend Wycliffe was nearly cheated of his prize." '

'Is that what he said?'

MacDonald arrived, a large, red-headed Scot. He looked at the major. 'What the hell has he been doing to himself now?'

Lane explained and the doctor made a brief examination. 'No surprises there. Usquebaugh – the water of life. Sadly you can have too much of it, especially with a dicky heart and after a set-to with an oil-stove.' The doctor was looking down at the major's body. 'Well, nobody can say he wasn't single-minded about killing himself one way or another.' He turned to Bunny Lane. 'If his house is burnt down it's no good taking him there so what do you suggest?'

Bunny said, 'I'd like him to stay here.' He looked doubtfully from the doctor to Wycliffe and back again. 'I don't suppose the three of us could get him into my little parlour? There's a bed there where my mother died. Towards the end she couldn't get up the stairs.'

MacDonald shrugged. 'You'll have to square it with that sister of his afterwards.'

'Give me a couple of minutes to get the bed ready.'

Bunny busied himself like an anxious housewife and ten minutes later when they carried the major into the parlour the brass bedstead had been made up with clean linen which smelt of lavender.

Bunny said, 'I'll ring Marty Jewel, the undertaker; he'll see to everything.' He gave Wycliffe a wry look. 'I'll leave him a key so that he can get in when I'm not here.'

After the doctor had gone and Bunny had spoken to the undertaker the two men sat in front of the fire in the living-room, smoking. The little clock on the mantelpiece showed half-past nine and Wycliffe checked with his watch before he could believe that only a couple of hours earlier he had been in his office.

Once or twice Lane opened his mouth to speak but thought better of it and said nothing. Then Wycliffe added casually, 'Did the major tell you what it was David Clement said which provoked him?'

Bunny shifted in his chair, 'It was what you'd expect; he referred to his brother, the major and me as "three addled old poufs".'

'I see.'

Another long interval of silence with Lane becoming increasingly uneasy at Wycliffe's passive attitude; no doubt he had expected that events having reached a crisis, the action would move swiftly to a climax. But Wycliffe sat and smoked, holding his pipe so that his hand covered the bowl.

His next question when it came seemed absurdly trivial. 'What about the Chippendale book? It was in Joseph's room.'

'I lent it to him earlier; I used it for an excuse . . . '

'I suppose it was you who drove the car and afterwards ditched it in the quarry?'

'Yes, then—'

'And you walked home?'

'Yes, I—'

'Just answer my questions; you will be asked to make a statement later.' Wycliffe's manner was curt, distant, authoritative.

The next question was a long time coming. 'You wanted it to appear that Clement had killed his brother and cleared out; wouldn't it have been more convincing if you had emptied the safe of money and valuables? You had the key.'

'I thought of that but the major wouldn't hear of it; he said we had no idea who the contents belonged to.'

A nice sense of morality, the major's.

'There were two paperweights worth about five thousand pounds in the pockets of Clement's bush-jacket.'

'They must have been there all along; we didn't put them there.'

Clement had probably slipped them into his pocket to keep them out of his brother's sight.

The little clock ticked away another couple of minutes. 'Did the major tell you that he intended to scuttle *Manna* in Porthellin Bay?'

'No, he simply said he knew a place where he could scuttle her without much risk of her being found and from where he could row ashore.'

'How did the gun come to be left on the beach?'

Bunny shook his head. 'I don't know; it happened while I was ditching the car. The major told me afterwards he'd dropped it while dragging the dinghy down the beach and couldn't find it again.'

'Did you believe him?'

'I'm not sure. The major was a strange man, never content unless the odds were against him.'

'Did he know it was his father's gun?'

'I don't know.'

At a quarter past ten by the little clock Wycliffe got up from his chair. 'I'm not taking you into custody. I want you to go to Mallet Street police station at nine o'clock in the morning and make a voluntary statement. You will be charged with being an accessory to the unlawful disposal of a body and brought before the magistrates. The police will not oppose bail. There could be other charges later . . . We shall have to see.'

Bunny stood up, incredulous. 'You mean I don't have to go with you?'

Wycliffe did not answer; he put on his mackintosh in

the little passage. Bunny opened the front door on the deserted square; it was a fine, clear night.

'Get yourself a good lawyer and tell him the truth.'

Helen was watching *Newsnight* on television and she switched off as he came in. She looked at him in a special way. 'Is the case over?'

His manner was surly. 'There was no case, only a wild-goose chase.'

Helen said, 'The paper says it was very clever of you to find the boat.'

'Too damned clever; it would have been better to have left her where she was.' He was on the point of adding, 'The major is dead, Hetty is in hospital and Bunny Lane . . . ' but there would have been too much to explain.

'I'll get you some supper. What about a bit of cold lamb with salad?'

'Anything.'

A quarter of an hour later when she came back with his tray he was sitting staring into the fire. 'Tomorrow night we are due at the Oldroyds' and we haven't made up our minds.'

Helen put the tray on a low table near his chair. 'I think we have.'

THE END

available from

THE ORION PUBLISHING GROUP

_____

Wycliffe and Death in Stanley
Street £5.99
W.J. BURLEY
0-7528-4969-7

Wycliffe and the Scapegoat
£5.99
W.J. BURLEY
0-7528-4971-9

Wycliffe in Paul's Court
£5.99
W.J. BURLEY
0-7528-4932-8

Wycliffe and the Quiet Virgin
£5.99
W.J. BURLEY
0-7528-4933-6

Wycliffe and the Tangled Web
£5.99
W.J. BURLEY
0-7528-4446-6

Wycliffe and the Cycle of
Death £5.99
W.J. BURLEY
0-7528-4445-8

Wycliffe and the Last Rites
£5.99
W.J. BURLEY
0-7528-4931-X

Wycliffe and the Guild of
Nine £5.99
W.J. BURLEY
0-7528-4384-2

Wycliffe and the Beales £5.99
W.J. BURLEY
0-7528-5872-6

Wycliffe and the Winsor Blue
£5.99
W.J. BURLEY
0-7528-5873-4

Wycliffe and Death in a
Salubrious Place £5.99
W.J. BURLEY
0-7528-6535-8

Wycliffe and the Four Jacks
£5.99
W.J. BURLEY
0-7528-4970-0

Wycliffe and the Dead Flautist
£5.99
W.J. BURLEY
0-7528-6490-4

Wycliffe's Wild-Goose Chase
£5.99
W.J. BURLEY
0-7528-6491-2

Wycliffe and How to Kill a Cat
£5.99
W.J. BURLEY
0-7528-8082-9

Wycliffe and the Guilt Edged
Alibi £5.99
W.J. BURLEY
0-7528-8083-7

CIRLS 5

All Orion/Phoenix titles are available at your local bookshop or from the following address:

> Mail Order Department
> Littlehampton Book Services
> FREEPOST BR535
> Worthing, West Sussex, BN13 3BR
> *telephone* 01903 828503, *facsimile* 01903 828802
> *e-mail* MailOrders@lbsltd.co.uk
> (Please ensure that you include full postal address details)

Payment can be made either by credit/debit card (Visa, Mastercard, Access and Switch accepted) or by sending a £ Sterling cheque or postal order made payable to *Littlehampton Book Services*.
DO NOT SEND CASH OR CURRENCY.

Please add the following to cover postage and packing

UK and BFPO:
£1.50 for the first book, and 50p for each additional book to a maximum of £3.50

Overseas and Eire:
£2.50 for the first book plus £1.00 for the second book and 50p for each additional book ordered

---

BLOCK CAPITALS PLEASE

name of cardholder ....

address of cardholder ....

....

....

postcode ....

delivery address
(if different from cardholder)

....

....

....

postcode ....

☐ I enclose my remittance for £................................

☐ please debit my Mastercard/Visa/Access/Switch (delete as appropriate)

card number ☐☐☐☐☐☐☐☐☐☐☐☐☐☐☐☐☐☐

expiry date ☐☐☐☐   Switch issue no. ☐☐

signature ....

prices and availability are subject to change without notice